AGAINST THE WALL

MONTANA MAVERICKS
BOOK ONE

REBECCA ZANETTI

RebeccaZanetti

To all of you who feel the pull of a cowboy's grin,
who are always ready to ride into a good story,
and who know that chaps aren't just for show—
this one's for you.

A SPECIAL THANK YOU

I want to extend my heartfelt thanks to Cathie Bailey from the Quapaw Tribe for her invaluable insights and thoughtful feedback on my story. Your perspective and generosity in sharing your knowledge enriched the narrative in ways I couldn't have achieved on my own. I'm deeply grateful for the time, care, and expertise you brought to this project, helping ensure the story resonates with authenticity and respect. Thank you for being part of this journey.

CHAPTER 1

*T*he silence bordered on bizarre.

Shouldn't there be crickets chirping? Birds squawking? Even the howl of a hungry wolf in the muted trees? Of course, such sounds would send a city girl like Sophie Smith barreling back through the trees to her rented Jeep Cherokee. The quiet peace had relaxed her into wandering far into the forested depths, but now the trees huddled closer together, looming in warning.

Enough of this crap. Time to head back to the car.

Her only warning was the crack of a stick under a powerful hoof, a thumping, and a shouted, "Look out!" A broad arm lifted her through the air. The arm banded solidly around her waist, and her rear slammed onto the back of a rushing horse. She yelped, straddling the animal and digging her hands into its mane. An image of the man attached to the arm flashed through her brain, while his rock-hard body warmed her from behind.

A cowboy.

Not a wannabe cowboy from a bar in the city. A real cowboy.

The image of thick black hair, hard-cut jaw, and Stetson hat burst through her shocked mind as muscled thighs gripped both the back of a massive stallion and her hips. The beast ran full bore over rough ground.

Only the sinewed forearm around her waist kept her from flying through the air.

This wasn't happening. Sophie shut her mouth on a scream as the powerful animal gracefully leaped over a fallen log and her captor pulled her into his solid body. He moved as one with the animal. Her hands fisted the silky mane like it was a lifeline to reality.

Maybe it was.

Screw this. She threw back an elbow and twisted to the side, fear and anger finally galvanizing her into action.

"Stop." A deep voice issued the command as warm breath brushed her cheekbone.

With a mere tightening of his thighs on the great animal, they skidded to a stop. The arm trapping her shifted so she slid easily to the ground and stayed around her waist until she regained her footing. With a sound that was more growl than gasp, she backed away from man and mount until she collapsed against the bark of a towering tree. The horse tossed his head and snorted at her retreat.

The man sat straight and tall on the animal, dark and curious eyes considering her.

The smell of wet moss surrounded her. She gulped in air and studied him. He was huge—and packed hard. Scuffed cowboy boots pressed down on the stirrups while a dark T-shirt outlined impressive muscles. Long lashes framed incredible eyes, and she could swear a dark eyebrow lifted in amusement.

Two more horses charged suddenly through the meadow, coming to a swift stop behind her captor. One animal was a pretty white, the other a spotted paint, and both held powerful cowboys complete with boots, jeans, and Stetsons. All wore black hats—like the villains in every Western movie ever filmed.

"Unbelievable," she muttered under her breath.

At her voice, her captor jumped gracefully off his mount and stepped toward her.

"What should we do with her?" the man on the white horse asked. His gravelly voice contrasted oddly with the glint of humor in his tawny eyes. Filtered sunlight illuminated the gold, brown, and even black hair flowing unchecked around his shoulders. He was a symphony of twilight, whereas the other men wore the ominous tone of midnight.

"I caught her. I get to keep her," her captor said, his eyes intent as he took another step toward her, firm muscles bunching in his arms.

"Another step, and you get to land on your ass." Sophie readied herself to target his knees as fear uncoiled in her stomach. He stood at least a foot taller than her own five foot four.

His grin was quick and unexpected. It also added to the nerves still jumping in her belly. He might be a psychotic throw-back to the pioneer days, but he belonged on a Calvin Klein underwear billboard.

The forest pressed in, and a smattering of pinecones hit the earth. Their soft, fragrant *thunks* shot adrenaline through her veins. Something high in the tree twittered a soft screech, reminding her she was far from home.

From safety.

She centered her breath and decided on a groin shot.

Just then, a happy feminine shout yanked her attention toward a petite young woman rushing toward the horses. The female whirlwind all but collided with Sophie's tormentor. "Jake, you're the best! I got the best picture ever. The action shots are amazing."

The woman released Jake and jumped at Sophie to grab both hands. "Didn't you hear them coming? They nearly mowed you down. But Jake has great reflexes—he saved you. The picture is phenomenal. Your eyes were huge, and you looked so scared! I am going to nail this project."

Sophie wrinkled her brow at the stunning woman. She had long black hair, straight features, and aquamarine eyes, which were alight with happiness as she pumped Sophie's hands in her own.

"You're welcome?" Sophie pressed her backside against the tree trunk.

The woman threw back her head and laughed. "I'm Dawn, and you already met my brother Jake." She gestured behind her to the motionless cowboy. "Those are my brothers, Quinn and Colton."

"Ma'am," both men said, tugging on hat brims while remaining perched comfortably on their stallions. Colton had the colorful array of hair, while Quinn's hair and eyes were as dark as Jake's.

Dawn stomped wet grass off her boots. "We're from the Kooskia Tribe. I was trying to capture an action shot, but you stepped right into their path. This was perfect." She patted Sophie's hand. "Don't worry. You weren't in any danger. Jake's an excellent rider."

Wait a freakin' minute. Sophie glared at Jake. What an asshole. "Why didn't you put me down sooner?"

"Sorry if we scared you," he said softly, his eyes anything but apologetic as his generous lips tipped in humor. "Dawn needed a picture for her college project while she and Colton are home for spring break, and I didn't want to stop until I was sure she'd gotten what she needed. It was a long setup—or so she told us."

Temper stirred at the base of Sophie's neck. *I caught her? I get to keep her?*

Colton chortled. "You should've seen your face."

"Yeah, you looked ready to faint," Quinn said as his horse tossed its head and sidestepped in a graceful prance.

"Actually," Jake said, his eyes narrowing, "she had shifted her stance to kick me in the knees." He cocked his head, almost seeming wishful she had tried it.

She wondered if she could've taken him down and ignored the annoying voice in the back of her head laughing hysterically.

"Really?" Colton smirked. "I would've liked to see that."

"Me, too." Sophie returned his amusement, and her temper dissipated. She bet she had looked terrified. She had been.

Dawn smiled even white teeth. "I'm a junior at the University of Montana, and for my photography project, I need to capture a series of action shots. There's nothing like horses rushing through shadowed trees to show action. Although, you're probably lucky Jake was able to pick you up before running you over."

Sophie cleared her throat, her gaze lifting again to Jake. Warmth spread through her abdomen. The man standing so solidly next to wild beasts and surrounded by untamed land was something new and definitely out of her experience. He was all male, and something feminine in her, deep down, stretched awake. Her heart kicked back into gear. Fighting her suddenly alive libido, she smoothed her face into curious lines. "Why didn't you just shout for me to get out of the way?"

He cocked his head to the side, those dark eyes softening. "I did, but you didn't move fast enough. One second the trail was clear, the next you were about to get trampled. I turned my horse and grabbed you before one of my brothers could run you over."

So he had actually saved her. Sure, he'd had some fun at her expense, but at least if she needed to kick him later for it, she still had legs. She lifted her chin. "Thanks for the rescue."

His cheek creased with a dimple before he turned and remounted his horse. "Any time, Sunshine."

"What were you doing on our land, anyway?" Dawn asked.

Sophie's heart dropped to her stomach. This was where the niceties stopped. "I'm Sophie Smith from Green Par Designs."

"Oh, the golf course lady." Dawn nodded.

That was an easy, accepting tone. Sophie frowned. "Yes. I'm here to design the golf course next to the lake, so I was checking out the land." Now the pretty woman would get angry, considering the Kooskia Tribe opposed the project. The pine-filled canopy blocked the sun's warmth, and Sophie shivered.

"Oh. Well, that explains it, then." Dawn tossed ebony hair out of her face.

Sophie gaped and quickly closed her mouth. "Aren't you opposed to the golf course?"

"Of course. For one thing, it's bad placement because the fertilizers will pollute the lake." Dawn softened her rebuke with a smile.

"And the other thing?" Sophie asked.

Dawn shrugged. "A golf course just doesn't fit the land right there."

"Doesn't fit?"

"Nope." Dawn tugged her toward the clearing. "Come on, I'll show you my shot before Jake takes you back to your car. Thanks again for the picture—it was perfect."

"You're welcome." Sophie shook her head and let the young woman lead her away while three muscled cowboys followed tamely behind them.

JAKE DREW IN AIR, his gut tightening as if Guardian had kicked him. Sophie's vanilla scent still wrapped around him. His hands itched with the desire to haul her back on the horse, but he contented himself with studying her head to toe.

Sunlight turned her mass of shoulder length curls to shiny wheat, the color both sweet and sassy. She was beautiful. Maybe not in the conventional movie-star way, more like a fierce "I'm going to knock you on your ass" way. He'd fought in combat, and he'd seen courage. The woman had shown bravery and brains when she'd faced him and settled her stance to fight. An irresistible combination.

At only an inch taller than Dawnie, Sophie was small. Faded jean capris cradled her sweet heart-shaped ass. An ass he'd love to dig his hands into. Her waist was tiny enough his arm had easily wrapped around it, and he couldn't forget the feeling of the full breasts resting just out of reach.

But those eyes.

They were the color of the deep blue irises his mama carefully tended each spring. And Sophie was a scrapper. She had been more than willing to try and knock him on his butt.

Quinn caught his eye, amusement lifting his lips.

Jake half shrugged. Yeah, he was checking out the city lady. The fierce look in Sophie's pretty eyes had contrasted nicely with her pale skin and classic features when she had prepared to take him down. As a lawyer, he enjoyed a good contrast. His groin hardened as he steered Guardian through the meadow. He'd love to wrestle with her.

She made the appropriate noises while looking through the viewfinder of Dawn's digital camera before his sister removed it and folded the tripod.

"I guess Jake will take you back to your car," Dawn said absently, handing the equipment up to Colton. Then she reached an arm to Quinn, who tugged her up to sit behind him on his pawing horse.

Jake fought amusement at the panic that rushed across Sophie's face.

"No, er, I'll just walk." She peered uncertainly around the clearing into the nearby trees, her pretty pink lips pursing.

"We came a lot farther than you think." Jake tried to sound reassuring. "I promise I'll go slow."

Sophie shook her head, sending blond curls flying. "Not a chance, sport. I'm walking." She turned and headed toward a trail barely visible between two bulky bull pines.

Quinn shrugged. "You're on your own. I have to get to work." He clicked his mount into a gallop, and he and Dawn took off, leaving Jake with Colton.

Sophie escaped between two trees.

"Do you think you can handle the pint-sized city girl, or do you need help?" Colton laughed as his horse danced impatiently to the side.

"The day I need help from you, shoot me, little brother." Jake tightened his knees on Guardian, who wanted to run again. Colton would have to return to graduate school in just a few days, and it didn't make sense to smack him around right now. "Get back to the ranch."

"With pleasure." Colton nodded toward the tree line. "You'd better get going. She just went the wrong way."

Jake pressed in with one thigh, turning the mount. Guardian plodded impatiently into the trees. Sophie came into view, picking her way carefully along scattered pinecones and exposed tree roots. Her spine straightened, and her shoulders firmed as he narrowed the gap between them, but she didn't acknowledge him otherwise.

Why did he like that about her? The woman was lost as a person could be, yet she marched forward into darkness. The trees soon thickened with prickly brushes and slash piles.

"You're going the wrong way," he said.

She came to an abrupt stop at his soft words.

Jake reined in Guardian, waiting for Sophie to turn around and face him. It took longer than he would have thought—stubborn was an understatement with the woman.

As she slowly turned, he could have kicked himself at the intelligent wariness in her gaze. She was alone in the middle of the nowhere with a strange man. He had a daughter, a little sister... He should've known better. They stared at each other, wildlife sounds surrounding them. Jake searched for the right words. "I won't hurt you. I just want to take you to your car."

Sophie lifted her chin but otherwise didn't move.

"I'll let you drive," Jake cajoled.

The smile that lit her pretty face warmed him. "There's no way I can drive that beast." She took a small step toward him.

"Sure you can." Jake reached down to offer an arm. He didn't question why it mattered that she trust him. It just did.

Vulnerability glimmered in her eyes. "Maybe we should walk instead."

He forced himself to relax, to appear as unthreatening as a guy twice her size could look.

Thunder rolled in the distance. Storm season had definitely arrived early.

He plastered his most earnest, trust-me, closing-argument expression into place. If the storm brought lightning, they'd need to dive for a ditch. The last thing he wanted to do was scare her. "Believe me, this is faster, and there's a heck of a storm coming."

Sophie eyed the darkening sky. With a deep breath, she stepped up to the quiet horse. "Okay, but we go slow. I mean, unless lightning starts to strike. Then we go fast. How do I get back on?"

The woman's bravery tempted him to haul her close, but he gave them both a moment as he shifted his weight. The thunder bellowed louder.

They only had minutes until the rain hit. He balanced himself with his thighs, reached down, and lifted her by the waist to perch in front of him. She fit nicely into his hold, and something clicked into place. "Relax," he whispered in her ear, placing her hands securely on the silky black mane. "If you're relaxed, the horse will relax."

"Right." Sophie coughed, and her muscles eased into something slightly less than rigor mortis.

"Okay, now grip the horse with your thighs, and tug him the way you want to go." Jake forced his libido into submission. The act was difficult, considering how tight his jeans had just become.

Sophie tugged, and Guardian shifted around to retrace his steps. "He's going," she whispered, her voice lowering in delight.

"Yep." Her voice was sexy as hell. The soft tenor shivered across his nerves. He hardened. *Basketball scores. Baseball stats. National holidays.* His mind reeled facts around in a futile effort to control his reaction.

Sharp pangs of light shot through the awning of pine needles and the rolling clouds. The horse meandered through the trees and past rambling huckleberry bushes. Jake let Sophie set the pace, and her muscles soon relaxed against him. Finally, they emerged out of the woods to the narrow dirt road where her Jeep waited.

Jake helped her to the ground.

She self-consciously stepped away and tossed curls out of her face. "Thanks for the lift," she said, backing up even more.

"Any time," he said.

"It was, ah, nice to have met you." She pivoted and bolted for her Jeep.

The woman wanted to be rid of him. He fought another grin. Too bad she wasn't going to get what she wanted—this time. She had no idea what was coming.

He waited until she jumped into the vehicle and watched until she drove out of sight, his heart lighter than usual as Guardian waited for the command to run.

CHAPTER 2

*I*n the dark night, several hours after her unexpected horseback ride, Sophie ran out to her rented vehicle to fetch her sketchpad and paused at seeing a folded note under the windshield wiper. Pausing, she looked up and down the quiet street and then back at the adorable bed-and-breakfast clapboard home, with its powerful porch light illuminating the entire area.

Silence, the calm and peaceful kind, surrounded her—except for a few crickets in the distance. Curiosity wandering through her, she reached for the paper, and unfolded it to read. *Get out of town before you get hurt.*

She blinked and looked around again, feeling nothing out of place. Whoever had left the message felt long gone.

Shivering anyway, she grabbed her sketchbook out of the Jeep and ran back inside the home and up to her room. What kind of coward would just leave a note like this? She rolled her eyes. If they thought that would scare her, they were crazy.

She tossed the note onto the dresser and changed back into her boxers and still warm T-shirt before slipping into the bed, careful not to disturb the papers scattered across the bedspread.

She loved the bed-and-breakfast with the burnished antique furnishings and lemon oil smell. The milk-glass lamp added to the moonlight from the open window, and needles from the massive bull pine outside scraped against the glass.

The peaceful surroundings washed away her unease as she glanced at the hastily scrawled note on the dresser. No doubt somebody was against the golf course project but didn't have the guts to confront her. So forget them. She shifted her attention to the legal documents her staff had faxed to her, and her head started to pound as she prepared for the early meeting with the Kooskia Tribe.

Her cell phone chattered a nameless tune, and she stretched to reach it.

"Hi, Sophia. How's life in the middle of nowhere?" The deep voice elicited a familiar fluttering in her lower stomach.

"Hi, Preston. I'm in Montana. I think it's somewhere." Accustomed to his using her full name, she settled more comfortably against the flowered pillows. "Why are you calling so late? Don't tell me your date had an early math test tomorrow." She chortled at her own joke as she imagined his blue eyes sparkling with humor.

"Funny. The blonde you met before leaving town works at Shinnies and isn't a college freshman. Do they even have running water where you are?"

"Running water, paved roads, and even electricity." Sophie lost her amusement at the image of the too-perfect waitress. "When are you going to stop dating bubble-headed Barbies?"

"When the right girl comes along, I guess."

The words hurt more than they should have. She reminded herself they were just friends. One freakin' kiss didn't make a relationship. She cringed as she thought of how distant he'd been afterward—at least until she reassured him they were just friends and the kiss had been a mistake.

"In fact," Preston's cultured voice reached across the miles,

"I've been thinking quite a bit about that kiss at the Christmas party."

Sophie focused all her attention on the little phone against her ear and struggled to keep her voice calm. "What kiss?"

Preston chuckled. "You know exactly what kiss."

Of course she did. She'd only relived the whole evening in her mind for months afterward. "I know. But Preston—"

"I can change, Sophia."

"I doubt that." She snorted even though her heart warmed. She'd had a crush on her debonair coworker for so long, she again wondered, *What if?*

"Well, I've done something..." Preston's voice lowered.

What in the world could he have done? "What?" she asked, keeping her voice level.

"I booked us on a Caribbean cruise next fall to celebrate your successful design."

She coughed. "That's a bit premature, isn't it? We don't even have the permit yet."

"You'll get it."

She wasn't so sure. "Wait a minute. What do you mean by 'us'?"

"I mean *us*. You and me. I'm tired of dancing around this. Your uncle is going to retire soon and wants the business taken care of. You and I have a comfortable relationship and it could be even better." Something clinked against the phone as he swallowed—probably his usual scotch in a crystal tumbler.

Her heart sank. She may have had a crush on the man, but her brain still worked. "Wow. Sounds like a successful merger."

"It would be. Add in the fact that we want each other, coupled with similar tastes and interests, I think we have it made."

"What about love?" she asked.

"Seriously? What are you, twelve years old?"

Sophie laughed. "Yeah, seriously. Shouldn't love, fire, passion...and all that be the goal?"

"Whose goal? Plus, we have the fire and passion, so love's probably just around the corner."

Sophie was quiet for a moment. Preston was exactly who she'd always wanted. Young, ambitious, already successful. He had even designed his own home overlooking the Bay in San Francisco, and he resembled a tall, blond, Nordic god. Plus, she genuinely liked him. "I don't know."

"Come on, Sophie. Be realistic and stop daydreaming—puppy love is for naive morons." Self-ridicule and an odd loneliness wrapped around his tone.

Her head jerked up. "Who hurt you so badly, Pres?" Her question surprised her even as she asked it.

Quiet reigned over the line. "I don't know what you mean." But he did. She could tell.

"Sorry. It just slipped out." So much for a routine phone call. For the first time, doubt filled her about the successful architect.

"It's all right." His voice hinted at sensual promise. "Also, I want to thank you for taking this project on so I could concentrate on the Seattle proposal."

She relaxed as they returned to business. "No problem. I've been waiting for Uncle Nathan to let me take the lead on a golf course design, and this is finally it." Of course, they'd only use her design if the county approved the construction plan. Hope inflated her chest.

"Yeah, I know. It's a big job. The Charleton Group stands to lose a boatload of money if this project doesn't come to fruition." The sound of paper shuffling came over the line. "More importantly, we have five more projects lined up with them. Our bottom line for the next three years depends on the Group."

"No pressure there," she muttered.

"Sorry. But you need to understand. We're in trouble."

The breath caught in her throat. "How much trouble?"

Silence echoed from a world away. Finally, Preston cleared his throat. "Your uncle met with financial restructuring specialists yesterday."

Holy crap. Sophie sat straight up. "We're going bankrupt?"

"That's one option," Preston said. "The economy has hurt us pretty badly. I think we can crawl our way out of this mess with your current project and mine in Seattle. They both need to work."

Her mind spun. Uncle Nathan couldn't lose the company. "Don't worry. I'll get the job here."

"Your uncle mentioned that the local tribe opposes the course," Preston said.

She picked at a thread on the bedspread, her shoulders hunching. "Yeah. That's why I decided to stay at the B and B on the reservation instead of in Maverick. I meet with the tribe tomorrow. They own the lake just below the proposal site and they're worried about pollution from fertilizer and people."

Preston sighed. "Our science is just as good as theirs, and the lake will be fine. But you still have to get the conditional-use permit with the county, and the tribe may have the influence to sway them."

Her skin prickled. "Yeah, I know. That hearing isn't until a week from next Monday, so I thought I'd see what headway I could make with the tribal elders tomorrow." She leaned against the pillows and forced her muscles to relax.

She loved to design but the legal issues involved in land-use planning caused a drumming in her temples. An ache between her eyes. A rolling in her stomach that forced her to take deep, measured breaths. "I don't understand why we need a permit from the county, since this is privately owned land."

"Well, the land is zoned rural, meaning you can put a house on every five acres. One of the possible uses is a golf course, but you have to obtain a conditional-use permit to proceed."

Preston took another deep swallow. "You need a public hearing in front of the county commissioners before they can make their decision. Sometimes those hearings get a bit, well, energetic."

"Great." Sophie ran through her schedule. "I meet with the Maverick Chamber of Commerce early next week as well as with a citizens' group concerned with development. Maybe having their support will help at the hearing."

"Sounds like a good plan. I'll let you get some rest before your big day tomorrow." What sounded like ice clinking in a glass clattered across the line. "Give some thought to my idea about our, er, personal merger. We'd be a good match."

Sophie started to reply when a loud beep came across the line.

"Oops, that's my second line. I'll talk to you later, Sophia." The line went dead.

Sophie powered down her phone and switched off the light. She stared at the muted ceiling. Moonlight glinted off the brass rail from the open window and lent a coziness to the room. Who would be calling Preston so late at night? Why would either of them be content to just have a good match in life? Was that what she wanted? Probably not. She wanted passion and desire and comfort. All feelings, no planning.

Her mother would be disgusted.

Sophie's thoughts flew again to the mad dash through the forest in the hard arms of a modern warrior. She had felt safe and protected in those arms even before she knew who he was or why he'd grabbed her. Even before she knew that she was, in fact, safe.

His eyes had shown interest—and promise. A fluttering winged around her abdomen that had nothing to do with her fear of horses and everything to do with the man who controlled wild beasts. Would she see Jake again?

Surprise filled her at how badly she wanted that to happen.

❧ ❧ ❧

JAKE PUT the truck in park, slipped the manila files into his briefcase, and tried to focus on tomorrow's hearing. It was a big one, and if he won the motion for his client, the opposition would settle. As a lawyer, he liked a good trial, but it was always better for a client to settle before all the stress started. Unlike him—he thrived on stress and the unexpected.

As a working single dad to a six-year-old, it was a good thing he enjoyed a challenge.

He stepped onto the gravel drive, his mind flashing to the pretty blonde who'd so bravely tried to steer his horse the previous day. Guts and beauty in such a small package was a temptation he'd never resist.

He glanced down at his watch. Damn it. He was late.

Why had he agreed to meet at the tribe's main lodge instead of in his office? He grimaced. He hadn't wanted Sophie to be uncomfortable, and the lodge was a thing of beauty. Next he was going to agree to her terms.

Which he couldn't do.

So he marched into the lodge and headed toward the main conference room, sliding inside the door.

The woman sat at the far end of the table, looking spring-fresh in a flimsy blouse and pencil skirt.

He loved a woman in a pencil skirt. She looked like every hot-librarian he'd ever dreamed about. "Miss Smith," he said smoothly.

Her eyes opened wide, her gaze sweeping from his boots to his suit. "What the heck?"

Amusement filled him, and he fought the insane urge to tug her from the chair for a kiss. "Not who you were expecting?"

Her eyes narrowed. "No. I was expecting a lawyer."

"I'm the tribe's lawyer." He couldn't help reaching for her

hand to shake. His palm enclosed hers, and he made sure not to squeeze the delicate bones.

"You're kidding me." She tugged her hand free, a pink flush wandering across her high cheekbones.

"Afraid not." He dropped onto the nearest chair, inhaling her fresh scent of strawberries and vanilla. "I've read over your proposal, and while I think the golf course is magnificent, it doesn't belong on the site you've chosen." Much better to get the business out of the way before he asked her out.

Sophie smiled then, and he felt his first sense of unease. Maybe this wouldn't be as easy as he thought.

⁂

AN HOUR AFTER MEETING HIM, Sophie wondered if she'd be arrested if she cold-cocked Jake Lodge across his arrogant face. "Mr. Lodge—"

"Jake," he reminded her. Again.

Sophie growled low in her throat. "*Jake*, you are not being reasonable."

"Yes, I am." Strong arms crossed over a hard chest as he sat back in the dark leather chair.

"Are not," Sophie spouted before she could stop herself. A raised eyebrow and glint of amusement met her frustration head-on. She took a deep breath. "You. Do. Not. Own. The. Land."

"I. Know. That." The amusement turned to a full-out grin. "I hate clichés."

"Excuse me?" she whispered.

"Clichés. They're boring." He placed two broad hands on the oak table between them and leaned forward, into her space. "But you are absolutely stunning when angry."

Her heart gave a nasty *thud*. Sophie shook her head. Even indoors the man was as primitive and dangerous looking as he'd been controlling a powerful stallion. His presence overwhelmed the small conference room with its tan leather chairs and burnished wooden table. Light filtered softly through several open windows, and the breeze carried the scent of wildflowers through the small room.

The scent of man tempted her much more than the flowers.

A long-sleeved black T-shirt emphasized strength and muscle, while faded jeans hung low on tight hips over his long legs. Black cowboy boots crossed negligently at the ankle, and he'd tied his dark hair back at the nape, throwing the sharp angles of his face into stark relief. Black eyes reflected humor and determination in equal parts as he held firm. The panoramic window behind him framed rugged mountains and a placid lake in gentle stillness.

The wildness outside only enhanced his.

His watchful intelligence made the floor beneath her pumps shift like quicksand. She smoothed curls back from her face and blinked to keep from glaring. "I thought I was meeting with a tribal elder today."

"You are, but the chief wanted me to explain our legal position to you first."

"You don't look like a lawyer." She said what she'd been thinking for the last hour.

Jake grinned an even row of white teeth. "Good. I'd rather you didn't see me as a lawyer."

"What do you want me to see you as?" Good Lord, she was flirting with the man.

The smile narrowed, and his dark gaze roamed across her rapidly warming face. "Hopefully someone you'd like to get to know better while you're in town, City Girl." His eyes hardened to deep coal.

"What?" She would've taken a step back had she been standing. As it was, her body tensed as she focused on the large man seated across the table from her.

The oak door behind Jake swung open, which prevented him from responding. An elderly man with long, shockingly white hair strolled into the room and crossed over to Sophie.

She rose to her feet.

His hands clasped hers warmly, and two dark brown eyes twinkled at her. "Miss Smith, I'm Chief Lodge of the Kooskia Tribe."

"It's nice to meet you, Chief Lodge." Sophie smiled up at a face similar to Jake's. Strong features set into a bronze face with lines created by laughter, although the sculpted jaw hinted at a stubbornness she'd already encountered in Jake, who had to be related. Charisma and charm surrounded the elder. If the chief was anything to go by, her new nemesis would age well. "Please call me Sophie."

"Ah, Sophie. Such a pretty name." The chief gestured for her to retake her seat as he turned and sat at the head of the table. He wore faded jeans over scuffed brown cowboy boots with a deep red button-down shirt. "I see you've met my grandson and lawyer, Jake."

"Yes." The warmth deserted her as she eyed Jake. His sparkling eyes made her want to throw something. At his head.

"So." The chief's upper lip quirked. "What can I do for you, Sophie?"

She focused on the elder's calm facade. Those deep lines sat comfortably on a smooth face—he could be anywhere between fifty and a thousand years old.

"I'm here to explain the golf course proposal and earn the support of the Kooskia Tribe." She hoped to have better luck with the him than she was getting from his grandson.

Wisdom flowed through the chief's eyes along with amusement. "Is that why you're here?"

"Um, well, yes." Sophie tossed a quick look to Jake. Did the chief know anything about her proposal or not?

"Oh, I've studied your design," the chief reassured her. "Sometimes what we think we know isn't what we really know." "I don't understand," she said.

The chief shrugged. "You don't need to." He reclined in his chair. "I have to tell you that your design is magnificent."

Sophie's eyes widened. "Really?"

"Yes. Wonderful—looks like a great course to play. I love to golf, you know," the chief said.

Sophie slanted a glance toward Jake, but his implacable face revealed nothing. She turned back to the chief. "The development will bring money to the tribe and casino."

"Yes, I believe that it would." He clasped broad hands together on the hard table. Hands that reminded her of Jake's. The breeze tossed the sweet scent of berries through the room as the chief breathed deep in appreciation. "Huckleberries. Should be quite the crop this year." He focused on Sophie's face. "They grow wild all over your client's property."

Sophie maintained her smile. "I understand that huckleberries grow wild across all the nearby mountains, even by the roadside."

The chief flashed an amused grin. "That they do. You're a spunky one, Sophie Smith."

"Thank you." Sophie ignored Jake's obvious amusement.

"The course really does look like a fun one. I especially like the water hazards." The chief nodded.

Her heart leaped into full gallop. "So you'll support the project?"

"Oh, no," the chief said sadly, still with a twinkle in his deep eyes. "I can't do that."

Even though she'd expected his rejection, a ball of dread slammed into her stomach. "May I ask why?"

"The golf course doesn't fit with the aesthetics of the land there," the chief said.

Not this again. "Of course it fits." Sophie kept the exasperation out of her tone.

"Nope." The chief gestured toward the north. "Have you surveyed the land in person?"

Sophie's spine straightened at Jake's quiet snort. "Um, no, not really."

The chief rose. "Well then, it's all settled."

"What's settled?" Sophie lurched to stand as well.

"Jake will take you tomorrow to inspect the land. You two can ride the northern ridge and enjoy a picnic overlooking the lake."

Jake started to protest as he took to his feet. "Grandpa." His chair echoed his annoyance as it slid back with a creak.

"That's an order from both the chief and your grandpa, boy," the chief said with a hard glint in his eye.

Jake turned to Sophie, his broad form blocking the sunlight streaming through the window. Humor creased his cheek, adding charm to the lethal angles of his face. "I'll pick you up at ten tomorrow morning."

"Wow." Sophie breathed. "Can you order him to stop being obnoxious and arrogant, too?"

Jake shot her a warning glance.

The chief roared out a deep laugh. "Sorry, Sophie. Those traits he inherited from his grandma's side." The elder chuckled as he ambled out the door.

"I am not going horseback riding with you." Sophie rounded on Jake and threw her hands in the air before leaving the conference room. Sure, she needed to explore the area to get a better idea for her design—just to make sure she'd covered all her bases. But she'd drive there.

"It appears you are, darlin'. Where we're going is only accessible via horseback. No vehicles." He moved silently, his scent of man and musk swimming over her as he reached the outside door and opened it.

Just wonderful. Now she needed to ride another horse.

Jake followed her out, and his broad hand at her lower back propelled her into sunshine. Natural pine scent filled the air, and gravel crunched underneath their feet. He walked her to the Jeep and opened the driver's door, his hands settling on her waist.

The gentle touch slid right under her skin, zinged around, and throbbed between her legs. She coughed. "I can get myself into my SUV."

He lifted her inside. "I know, but my mama taught me to be a gentleman."

Sophie swallowed. "That wasn't gentlemanly."

His chuckle caressed her skin as if his tongue traced each inch. "I didn't say I was good at following the lessons." His hands lingered on her waist, and his midnight dark eyes caressed her heated features.

Sophie tried to ignore the strength in the hands at her hips. He had lifted her into the Jeep like she weighed nothing. His broad chest blocked the building behind him. In fact, all she could see were those onyx eyes devouring her. Interest and something even darker lurked there. Flutters cascaded through her belly.

The man wanted to kiss her.

Why wait? Feeling reckless and against all logic, she leaned up and pressed her mouth to his.

CHAPTER 3

*J*ake took her invitation and captured her lips, the jolt of instant lust shocking him. The attraction between them was obvious and something new. Something intriguing.

So he forced himself to slow down and explore softly, gently, at his leisure. He wasn't a man who lost control. Ever.

One hand cupped her head, holding her where he wanted her. Her eyes closed, and he took the kiss deeper, his nerves exploding as heat shot through his blood. His gentle hold kept her firmly in place as he controlled them both.

Desire and a shocking intimacy careened through him. Under his touch, the woman stilled, no doubt fighting to keep sane. It was too late for sanity. Way too late. With the hint of a growl, his tongue invaded her mouth. He took his time learning her texture, memorizing her taste. The hand at her nape threaded into her hair, and he let them both get lost.

She clenched his shirt and slid her tongue against his.

Fire boiled through him, and his groan of approval filled her mouth. His hand caressed from her waist and relaxed against her thigh, her toned muscle tempting him to yank the material away. Then he pulled her closer, and her breasts flattened against his chest, her nipples pebbling.

Lava cascaded down his spine to spark his balls. He wanted her naked. Now.

Obviously, the woman had no clue how close to the edge he'd slipped. She burrowed farther into his body, returning his kiss. They both panted wildly when he finally lifted his head.

Her eyes had darkened to dangerous blue depths, wide and unseeing on his.

He released her curls before stroking along her jaw to cup her chin. He watched the path of his thumb as it ran along her swollen bottom lip. Tempting. Too damn tempting. Her tongue slipped out and grazed his thumb.

He bit back a growl and forced himself to relax. They were fully clothed, in a parking area next to headquarters, and he'd never wanted a woman more. But this was neither the time nor the place. *Definitely* not the place.

At that second, seeing the promise in her pretty eyes, he knew he'd have her –without question. But he wanted all night from dawn to dusk to explore whatever this was.

Awareness flitted across her face, and she yanked her hands away, turning to face the steering wheel. "I, ah, have to go."

He'd grant her a brief reprieve. Jake leaned in and pulled the seat belt between her breasts before clicking it firmly in place. "Go ahead and run, Sunshine. I caught you once before." The door closed, but he made sure she could still hear him. "I will again."

AFTER A SLEEPLESS NIGHT where he couldn't stop thinking about kissing Sophie, the morning sun poked through a light gauze of clouds while Jake maneuvered his truck across town.

"Why can't I come on the picnic and meet the golf course lady?" The litany of questions continued from the backseat.

Jake drove the pickup around a pothole, then glanced in the rearview mirror and met irritated feminine eyes. Eyes so much like his own. "Because you have plans to bead necklaces with your grandmother, pumpkin."

"I don't wanna bead necklaces. I wanna go on the picnic." Annoyance turned to sweetness. "Please, Daddy? I want to meet the city lady."

"Nice try, Leila." His grin matched hers.

Her expression turned dreamy. "I bet she has Manolo Blahniks."

"Manolo what?" He turned down a narrow dirt driveway lined with lodge pole pines.

"Ah, Dad," Leila huffed in pity. "Blahniks. Shoes. Really pretty shoes."

"You're six years old. Since when do you care about shoes?"

Leila's midnight black eyes widened before she gave a delicate shrug and stared intently out the window.

Awareness ticked down his spine. What in the world was she hiding from him now? "Leila?" He used his best no-nonsense tone. The one that promised a lack of ice cream in the future if she didn't answer.

Leila slowly looked back to meet his gaze. "Since me and Grets and Sally watched *Sex and the City*."

Jake gaped at his daughter. His baby with her long dark hair pulled into two pigtails and her pert little nose. "*Sex and the City?*"

"Yep." The sweet smile showed a gap from a missing tooth.

Jake's lips tightened. "Where?"

Leila plucked at a string on her shirt. "At Sally's house after school last week."

"Her mother let you?"

She shrugged one tiny shoulder. "Well, not zactly."

"Meaning?" He stopped the truck before a two-story log home surrounded by wild purple, yellow, and red flowers. He shifted in his seat to face his daughter. She appeared innocent and pretty in her blouse and light jeans with tiny tennis shoes.

A guilty flush stole across Leila's face in a light pink hue. "Um, well, her mom thought we were watching a cartoon about kittens in her room, but we kind of put in the other movie instead."

"I will call Madeline later today so she knows what you three were up to," Jake said sternly before jumping from the truck and opening the back door. He released the seat belt and helped his daughter out of her booster seat before shaking his head. "You get no television for a week."

"A week?" Leila wailed just as Jake's mother opened the door and gracefully crossed the faded deck.

"Want to make it two?" he asked.

Leila took off at a run toward her grandma the second Jake put her on her feet. "No."

Jake turned in exasperation as the two women in his life embraced.

"Daddy's being mean," Leila whined.

"Men," his mother agreed, a twinkle in her dark eyes.

Jake gave her a warning glance before stalking over and kissing her weathered cheek. His mother was truly a beautiful woman. Nearly a foot shorter than him, petite, and slender, she had passed on her black eyes as well as her straight, patrician bone structure, whereas he had inherited his broad frame from his father.

The braid through her gray hair deserved a tug, and Jake complied.

"Why are you picking on my granddaughter?" She smacked his arm.

"Because your granddaughter watched *Sex and the City* last week."

"Oh my." Loni Freeze bit her lip while turning to his urchin. "Why did you watch that?"

"To see the pretty clothes. And shoes. And the big city with the big stores and buildings." Leila clapped her hands together.

Jake's gut rolled at her words. "The city isn't everything it's cracked up to be, Leila."

"Jake, all girls dream of big stores in pretty cities," his mother chided.

"I'm well aware of that," he replied grimly. And he was. He and Leila had lost too much due to the lure of urban life.

His thoughts flashed to Sophie. Even her name screamed sophistication. He couldn't believe that he'd kissed her. What had he been thinking? A slow grin ripped across his face. He wanted to do it again.

His mother's eyes narrowed thoughtfully. "You have that look."

"What look?" he asked, all innocence.

"That look. The one you had right before riding that untamable stallion, Satan. Incidentally, does your arm still ache before a storm?"

Jake didn't answer.

"The look you had when your brother dared you to jump off Smitty's cliff into the lake." His mother continued with a huff. "The look you had when—"

"All right. I know the look." The smile deserted his face. "I don't have it right now."

His mother opened her mouth to speak, only to have Leila interrupt. "Where's Grandpa Tom?"

"He's mending fences in the south pasture. He'll be back in time for lunch with you," Loni assured her granddaughter.

Jake frowned. "Mending fences? Why didn't he call?"

"Because"—Loni reached up to peck him on a cheek—"your stepfather is just like you. He doesn't ask for help."

Jake nodded toward his daughter. "I ask for help."

"Humph," Loni replied with a twinkle. "Shouldn't you get going on your date?"

"It's not a date," he said.

She shrugged. "I heard it's a date."

"Your father had better not be matchmaking, Mom."

"I have no control over *your grandfather*." A smile lit her pretty face. "Have you noticed that we never quite claim him?"

Jake glanced at his watch. "No. I have to get going—for my *business meeting*." He emphasized the last two words before swooping down to kiss his daughter on the head before stalking toward his rig.

His mother's voice stopped him just as he reached the truck. "Maybe it's time to date again."

"Maybe," he allowed with a cautious glance at his suddenly curious daughter. "But not some city girl with Manolos. Whatever the heck those are." His gaze narrowed at his mother, who had an arm around his child. The homestead sat strong and solid behind them. Happy whinnies cascaded out of the deep green paddocks to the south, while the scents from steers to pasture wafted around.

Dust, dirt, and nature commingled into a combination of *home*.

With a shake of his head, he tossed his black Stetson across the front seat and jumped into the truck to meet the woman he'd kissed. A woman who belonged on his dusty ranch as much as a stallion belonged on Park Avenue. But first, he had a stop to make.

He drove through town to the general store, dodging inside to make his purchase. Within fifteen minutes he was back in the truck heading toward the edge of town, wondering when his daughter had stopped watching cartoons. His thoughts still whirled when he wiped his black boots on the mat adorning Shiller's B and B's large porch, removed his hat, and knocked on the door.

Sophie opened it immediately, fresh and pretty in dark jeans, frilly white blouse, and a braid seeming too similar to his mother's.

"These are for you." Jake handed her a large white box. Roses came in big white boxes, and he wondered belatedly if she'd be disappointed. They weren't flowers.

Sophie stuttered in surprise as she accepted the box. She flipped open the lid and stilled. "You brought me boots?" Her face wrinkled in confusion.

"Yeah. They're not Manolos." Jake shuffled his boots. "Plain old cowboy boots, and you'll need them for your ride today."

"They're beautiful," Sophie breathed out. Soft calfskin leather colored a creamy beige with a pointed toe. She hurried over to the wide porch swing covering one side of the wrap-around porch and slipped off her tennis shoes.

"Dawnie picked them out. She had to guess at the size." Thank goodness his sister had time between classes to help him out.

"They're perfect," Sophie said after yanking both boots up under her jeans. She stood, the boots giving her a couple inches in height. "But I can't accept them." Regret colored her words to reflect in her blue eyes.

Jake grinned. He couldn't help it. What was it with women and shoes? Sophie looked like she was about to cry at giving up the boots. "Montana law, ma'am," he said.

"Huh?" Her brow wrinkled more.

"Montana law. A representative of the bar association, *me*, gives an associate boots, *you*, then state law dictates you have to keep them," he said.

Sophie laughed and shook her head. "Really?"

"Really," Jake affirmed solemnly.

"No, Jake—"

If he had to charm her into accepting the gift she so obviously wanted, then no problem. "Please, Sophie? You're probably used to more lavish gifts, but I really want you to have them."

She gazed in wonder at her pretty new boots. "I'm not used to gifts at all. Thank you. These are perfect." She balanced up on her toes and back down like a graceful ballerina.

"You're welcome," he said thoughtfully. How odd. Why wasn't she accustomed to receiving gifts? "I don't suppose you know how to ride a horse?"

Sophie's gaze flew to his face. Her partial lesson the other day on his horse probably didn't count. "Um, not exactly…"

CHAPTER 4

*T*oo soon, Sophie found herself perched on a mammoth animal. "All right, Mertyl, you sweet girl— slow and easy," she crooned to the painted mare, her entire body tense and expecting to hit the ground. Eyes forward, Mertyl plodded ahead with a bored snort. At least, it sounded like boredom.

Thick pine trees unfolded lush branches on either side of the dirt trail as a woodpecker beat a sharp staccato tune somewhere high up. Orange honeysuckle and thick huckleberry bushes fought for dominance throughout the trees, their sweet scents mixing with sharp pine. A cool breeze wafted through the sharp sunlight angling through branches and brought peace to the area.

They truly were alone.

Sophie fought to relax her butt and thigh muscles as she balanced. She couldn't help but remember Jake's hard thighs bracketing hers on the big black horse he rode again today. She studied his broad back as he maneuvered a ton of near-wild animal along the old trail easily, naturally.

Today he was all cowboy in faded jeans, black Stetson, and

boots, his hair tied back at the nape. He was even bigger than she'd remembered. A dark gray shirt emphasized the breadth of a muscular chest that her body remembered well.

Her gaze softened as one of her new boots caught her eye. He'd bought her boots. Then she shook her head. He was a cowboy. A lawyer, no less. If that wasn't bad enough, his main job was to prevent her from doing hers. She needed to remember they were opponents in a battle about to begin. A battle that could determine the rest of her career and save her uncle's company. Boots or not.

As the trail angled upward, Sophie had to admit Jake had been correct about her horse. Slow and steady. Pretty safe. Mertyl had looked almost grateful when Jake led her from the deep rust-colored paddock on his ranch. Sophie had admired the color of the building, and Jake explained it matched his parents' paddocks, since he'd wanted consistency throughout all the ranches. His warm tone illustrated a closeness with his parents.

She had looked around for his home, but several mature blue spruce trees down the private driveway hid it.

Suddenly, the lake sparkled as the trail broke into a clearing of trampled wheat and sagebrush surrounded large rocks baking in the sun. Thick trees encircled the vista on three sides while a steep incline led down to the water far below.

Jake jumped lithely off his stallion near the edge of the trees, turned, and reached to lift Sophie from Mertyl. His hands remained warm and strong around her waist as she regained her balance and stretched already protesting muscles. He waited until she met his gaze.

"That wasn't so bad, was it?" Amusement wove through his tone.

Her heart accelerated as his midnight eyes ran over her face in an almost physical caress. Sophie shook her head. She'd agreed to the trip so she could see her client's land from a different perspective, not to flirt with the sexy lawyer. So she stepped back, and he released her.

Sophie turned toward the lake, letting its placidness calm her nerves while Jake tied reins to trees before grabbing two backpacks slung over his horse. He deftly shook out a tightly woven blanket with white, red, and brown-stitched patterns and spread it on the ground before adding plates, containers of food, and a bottle of wine.

"You really come prepared." Sophie sat gingerly on the beautiful blanket.

A dimple flirted in his left cheek as Jake opened the containers. "My daughter helped pack the essentials."

She blinked. "You have a daughter?"

"Yeah." Pride shone in his deep eyes. "Leila. She just turned six."

"Pretty name," Sophie murmured. Caution stiffened her spine. "You're not, I mean, you're not married, are you?" The heated kiss from the previous afternoon flashed through her mind.

Pain stamped down hard on the sharp angles of his face. "No. My wife died when Leila was only two."

"I'm sorry." It wasn't enough.

"Me, too." He handed her a plate before opening the wine.

An orange-breasted robin hopped closer to the blanket, its beady eyes on the feast. "How did she die, Jake?" Sophie asked.

He handed her a glass of chardonnay. "She died running away from me." He effectively ended the conversation by passing her a container filled with fried chicken.

They ate in silence. Sophie wondered about his deceased wife but didn't want to dampen the afternoon with sadness. She'd ask later.

"It's so peaceful here," She mused as two more robins joined the first.

"Yes. Without a golf course," Jake said dryly.

Sophie tossed her empty plate into a garbage sack. "Golf courses are peaceful places. At least if they're designed correctly."

"Not the same, Soph." Jake gestured at the deep green lake below them. "The risk isn't worth it."

Irritation jangled her nerves. "The golf course won't pollute your lake."

"The science doesn't confirm that. Again, it's not worth the risk. Besides, you don't own any of the land, do you?"

She exhaled slowly, holding on to her temper. "No. A private company owns the land. They hired us just to design the golf course." The sun beat down, and she inhaled the crisp air.

"Well then, maybe we're on the same side here," he said.

Sophie rolled her eyes. "Is this when I notice that a golf course doesn't belong here?"

Jake reached out one broad arm and yanked Sophie down beside him to face the clouds. "The land has been whispering since you arrived. You just need to listen."

Sophie quieted with her head on Jake's muscled shoulder, her face turned to the sky, her back comfortable against the blanket. She really should get up. Or move away. But he was so warm, so solid. She ignored her inner voice and shut her eyes to listen.

A breeze scattered pine needles to the hard earth. Honeysuckle layered the wind with sweetness. Birds twittered to each other in song, and Jake breathed deep and sure next to her. She opened her eyes.

Clouds drifted lazily across a beach-warm sky as a sense of peace slipped through her bones into her deepest marrow. "I think a golf course would still be peaceful here."

"Why aren't you used to presents, Sophia?" he asked.

The wind brought a chill, and Sophie snuggled closer into Jake's side. Just a bit. "Ugh. Please don't call me that."

"What's wrong with Sophia?" Laziness coated his deep voice as he stared upward.

Embarrassment heated her cheeks. "It's pretentious. I mean, seriously. 'Sophia Smith'? What was she thinking?"

"Your mother?" he asked.

Unease settled in her stomach. "Yeah."

"Is she French?"

"No, she wasn't French. She just wanted to be somebody." And she'd reached her goal.

"*Wasn't* French?" he asked.

Remembered hurt slithered down Sophie's chest. "She and my stepfather died in a car accident when I was eighteen."

"She was somebody."

Sophie pushed old hurts out of her mind. "How do you figure?"

"She was your mother," he said.

Sophie's shoulders tensed. "That wasn't enough, believe me."

"I still don't understand." He tucked her closer.

Sophie let out a deep breath. "I'm not sure she knew who my father was. If she did, she never said. We were poor. Trailer-park poor. She always wanted more."

"Did she get it?"

"Yeah. She married my stepfather, Roger Riverton, when I was fourteen. Then she got to travel everywhere."

"What about you?" he asked.

Sometimes loneliness snuck up and chilled her skin, like now. "Boarding school. It was all right, I guess."

"Did you like him? Your stepfather?" Jake's deep voice wound nicely through the silence.

"Not so much. He was quite a bit older and had already raised his family. In business, well, he was ruthless," she murmured.

Jake ran a hand down her arm, as if to offer warmth and reassurance. "How did you know he was ruthless?"

Memories flashed, bringing a dull ache to her temples. "A girl at school told me. I guess Roger raided her dad's company and then tore it apart. It's what he did." She watched the clouds drift. "Once a man came to visit when I was home for school break. He was almost crying, practically begging Roger not to destroy his family's construction business. I shouldn't have listened at the door, but..."

Jake tightened his hold. "What happened?"

"Roger didn't care. He was so cold, so *mean*. Like a shark. He told the man to forget it, that he deserved to lose his company. That he was weak." She shivered. "That's how Roger made so much money."

"Some of the money went to something good, right? I mean, to your schooling?" Jake asked.

Sophie tightened her jaw. "No. When they died, everything went to his kids. I had a scholarship to school and took out some loans, so it all worked out." She had never wanted Roger's money.

Jake was quiet for a moment. "How did you choose golf course design?"

Sophie laughed, her heart lightening. "I loved art. Drawing and creating. When I met Uncle Nathan, Roger's brother, he helped me channel that into design. He's my boss now."

"Ahh. You love him," Jake said.

"Yes. When I was younger, I used to wish he was my dad. That Mom had married him instead." Sophie rolled onto her stomach to face Jake. His muscles were relaxed, and he had one hand behind his head. "What about you? Are your parents still living?"

"My mother is. My father died in a snowmobile accident when I was eight and Quinn was six." Jake's eyes darkened.

Sophie reached out to pat Jake's chest. "I wondered about Colton and Dawn. They look different from you and Quinn."

Jake's eyes crinkled. "Yeah. Mom married Tom a couple of years later and then they had Colt and Dawnie."

"Were you upset she remarried?"

"Not really. I mean, he isn't Kooskia, so I wasn't so sure for a while. But Tom's great, and he makes Mom happy. Though Dawn…" Jake's gaze narrowed. "She has been a handful. For all of us."

"Three older brothers? Poor Dawn." Sophie couldn't imagine having three older brothers. "Is it important to you? I mean, was Leila's mother a member of the tribe?"

"Yes. She was full Kooskia," Jake said.

For some unknown reason, his admission deflated her.

Then he frowned. "I thought being a tribe member was important—that we'd want the same things."

"But you didn't?"

"No." The color of Jake's eyes deepened, and his hand slid to the back of Sophie's head.

She placed both hands against his chest and pushed to a seated position. "No way. No more kissing."

"Why not?" Jake sat up, his eyes intent on her mouth.

Despite her resolve, heat flared in her abdomen. "Because this is business. We're on opposite sides."

"We don't have to be." His voice deepened to a husky tone.

"Yeah, we do." Her brain told her body to get a grip. "Unless you're going to support my design?"

"No." Regret colored his words.

They were on opposite sides, no matter how sexy he was or how much she wanted to kiss him again. "We should get back." She shivered as the wind caught a chill.

His gaze ran over her face. Then he nodded and rolled to his feet, holding out a broad hand to help her up. "Yeah, we should. The spring storm season should be arriving any day, and while impressive, you don't want to be caught outside."

"Spring storm season?" She moved to help him repack.

"Yes. Probably not until next week, though the breeze coming off the lake has more of a chill than it should." He turned and lifted her onto the mare, helping her insert her new boots in the worn stirrups.

Sophie felt slightly more at home on the pretty horse, but while her body relaxed, her thoughts spun. What had he meant that his wife had run away from him? How had she died? What would it be like to kiss Jake again? Maybe the first time was just a fluke. It didn't matter that she wasn't Kooskia—one silly kiss didn't mean anything.

What she needed to concentrate on was how she could convince Jake to change his mind and help her earn the tribe's support for her proposal.

They arrived back at the paddock before she knew it. Jake's indulgent groan as they drew closer should have provided warning to whom obviously awaited them.

"Hello, Sophie." Chief Lodge strolled out the big double door.

"Afternoon, Chief Lodge." Sophie gratefully took his offered hand and swung down from the horse. Her leg muscles protested in a spasm, and she stumbled.

"Did you see the land?" The chief steadied her until she could stand on her own.

She put both hands on her hips and stretched her back, ignoring the loud pop from the base of her spine. "Yes, I did survey the land."

"And?" the chief asked.

"I think a golf course would fit perfectly in that spot." She grinned at the elder.

The chief threw back his head and guffawed. "Oh, Sophie, you're a pip." He wiped his eyes with one gnarled hand. "That settles it, then."

Her entire body revolted from her earlier ride. "Settles what?"

"You have to attend the branding picnic tomorrow, out at Rain's," the chief said.

"Grandpa..." Jake swung from his horse to stand at her side.

She threw a disgruntled look his way. *His* muscles seemed fine.

"There now, Jake agrees. We need to be there early, but I can give you directions." The chief patted her on the back. "Besides, the entire tribal council will be there, so you can talk to all of them about your proposal."

She chewed her bottom lip while flicking another glance toward Jake. It would be nice to speak with the entire council, so maybe she should go. Though the frown on his sexy face didn't warm her heart any. "Well, I'm not sure."

"Saturdays are meant for fun, so you must come." The chief offered her an arm. "Now, why don't we let Jake take care of the horses, and I'll give you a ride back to Shiller's B&B."

"Oh, er, okay." She'd grab any opportunity to sell him on her plan. Taking his proffered arm, she gave Jake a small smile over her shoulder. "Thanks for the picnic."

"No problem, Sophie. I'll see you tomorrow," Jake said.

Why did that sound like a threat?

CHAPTER 5

*A*fter a quick trip to the general store, Sophie spent the rest of the day fine-tuning her proposal, her muscles protesting the earlier horse ride. She ignored the new message she'd found on her windshield outside the local market. This time the statement had been more explicit: *Your development will destroy the land—rethink your plan or you'll regret it. Please think twice.*

At least the anonymous person had asked nicely this time. She placed the note with the first one, wondering if she should file a police report. The last thing she wanted was to appear like a hysterical female—and the messages weren't exactly threats. They were more like pleas. Nice, polite pleas. She could handle this. The tribe was against the development, but she couldn't imagine Jake leaving a cowardly threat for her. He was more likely to beat down her door to object to the proposal.

She ate a quiet dinner with Mrs. Shiller, the sole proprietor of the B&B. After helping clear the dishes, she escaped to her room and the purchases she'd been thrilled to find in the general store. She pulled out a new sketchpad and charcoals from the brown bag. They were beautiful, untouched, and ready to be used. The charcoal felt warm and solid in her hand as it vibrated with possibilities. The blank sheet before her called for something, so she reached out to create.

Her first drawing captured the clearing where they'd picnicked with its amazing view of Mineral Lake, tall pine trees and bouncing robins. Flecks in the rocks sparkled in the hazy sunlight as wispy clouds stretched toward the ground. The movement of charcoal against paper calmed her; even the smell of charcoal dust inspired her to continue.

Her second drawing took hours as she lost herself in every line and shadow. About midnight, she stretched her aching neck and scrutinized her work while spraying a light coat of fixative over the paper. Her nerves hummed as Jake stared unapologetically back at her from the paper, his eyes warm and serious, his cheekbones sharp angles over dark hollows, and his mouth full and slightly tipped. Black hair cascaded away from a broad forehead—strength and power flowed through every line across his face.

He was perfect.

And he wasn't hers to draw.

Her cell phone shattered the peace and she jumped, dropping the sketchpad and checking the number. Preston. She thought about his offer. Nope. Not dealing with him tonight. She muted the phone and went to bed.

The hours spent drawing had calmed her to the point that she fell asleep easily. She dreamed a dark, dreamless sleep until the early morning hours, waking up with decent energy. It must be the mountain air.

She pushed snarled curls off her forehead and swung her feet over the bed. The cold wood floor forced a chill up her legs, and she darted to her suitcase for socks and a comfortable cardigan. Her eye caught the soft light filtering through the silk curtains—and the clock. She gasped as she noted the time—she'd better hurry. What did one wear to a branding party?

With a shrug, she donned dark jeans and a light purple blouse, fetching a sweater in case the weather turned. A quick swipe of mascara and a clip to contain her curls finished the look. After pulling on her new boots, she secured the chief's directions in one hand and darted out the door.

Once in the Jeep, she sat for a moment. With an irritated grumble, she jumped out of the car and ran to fetch her sketchbook. She was going to be late.

The directions were simple. Sophie drove through town and turned left at Rain's Crossing. Soon enough, freshly painted white fences lined both sides of the road where horses ranging from light tan to colorful paints frolicked to the right, while steers and cows dotted the field to the left. She'd have to return when she had more time to sketch the placid scene of contrasting colors.

She pulled in behind a green Ford pickup beside a trio of large brown cows chewing grass in their large mouths, only separated from her by a wooden fence. Sophie gave the three an uneasy smile before following the line of trucks up a slight hill. She stopped at the rise and surveyed the ranch below. To the left of a large two-story log-planked house, colorful picnic tables perched among the trees near a large bunkhouse. Several barns, paddocks, and fenced areas stood to the right, as did most of the crowd.

Her boots clomped a rhythmic tune down the hill, toward the sounds of hooting and hollering. Several people stood on or by a three-slatted white fence, shouting encouragement. She spotted Dawn standing on the bottom rail of the sturdy fence and made a beeline for her new friend. She had just placed one foot on the bottom rung when a cheer rose from the spectators.

"This way, Colt!" a man called from inside the square corral.

She knew that voice. Awareness fluttered in her stomach at hearing Jake's deep baritone. She shifted up to see over the top rung.

Good God. The man was wearing chaps.

Actual chaps.

Jake's worn cowboy hat perched atop a grimy forehead as sweat ran in rivulets down his dirty face. Mud and dust caked his black shirt, and light jeans poked through the deep brown chaps protecting his legs. He dug scuffed cowboy boots into the earth while twisting two large horns in his leather-gloved hands, rolling a massive steer to the ground. Jake's face set into hard lines of determination as he battled the beast.

The steer bellowed when Jake shifted to press one firm knee into its neck, his hands pressing the horns to the ground, effectively immobilizing the animal's body. Colton rushed in with a needle and inoculated the animal just before another man pressed a hot iron to its flank.

The stench of burning fur filled the air in tune with the steer's protest. Jake released him and jumped back. The steer leaped to its feet and ran out a narrow side exit into another pasture. The beast had to weigh at least a ton, maybe two. Fortunately, the pen safely kept the spectators from danger.

Jake grimaced at Colton across the dusty pen, his dimple winking through the grime. "It's your turn to roll 'em to the ground." He yanked off his hat and wiped his forehead with one muscled arm.

"But you're so good at it," his brother returned, his face caked with mud.

Sophie stood in shock as warmth pooled deep in her belly. She was so completely out of her element. Yet what a display. She had never seen such masculinity before.

Man against beast.

And man won.

Jake was filthy. Covered in dirt and who knew what else.

The urge to kiss him again tempted her. Her mother would be shocked.

His dark gaze found her, and she forgot all about her mother. She may have forgotten how to breathe. Then he smiled and she forgot how to think.

"Well hello, Sunshine." He pounded his cowboy hat on his chaps and dust flew as he stalked toward her. "You look pretty today." Then his dimple winked again. "I like your boots." He stopped just on the other side, eye-to-eye with her as she stood, riveted, on the fence rung.

"Me, too." Heat flushed into her face. "They're my favorites."

"You wear them well." Something unidentifiable flashed through his eyes. For some reason, his look streaked heat through the rest of her. "Are you going to eat lunch with me?" The dimple returned.

Her eyes fixed on his mouth. "I didn't bring any food."

"I brought enough for both of us." The sound of another steer prodding toward the pen echoed behind him. "I have about ten more to do before lunch." He turned back just as the beast rushed into view. "Dawnie, tell Sophie the rules for watching," he called over his shoulder, his attention on the animal.

Dawn tipped back her cream-colored cowboy hat and gave Sophie a big smile.

"Rules?" Sophie muttered.

"Oh yeah, there are always rules, trust me," Dawn said with a practiced eye roll. "Basically, if a steer comes your way, take three steps back."

Sophie rubbed dust off her wrist. "Why?"

"Well, we haven't had one bust through the fence in a while, but it has happened," Dawn said.

Three steps? Man, she'd run for the car. "Okay."

"So how was your date?" Dawn asked.

Now Sophie rolled her eyes. "It wasn't a date. It was business."

"Right." Dawn straightened. "Colton, watch your left," she yelled just as the steer turned its head.

Sophie gasped as Colton shifted to the left, narrowly missing being gouged. "Good thing you're here to watch your brothers," she said quietly.

Dawn nodded toward the third man in the pen. "I'm here to watch Hawk."

"Hawk?" The name fit. Thick black hair was cut short above a face too sharp to be rugged. Deep green eyes watched the steer as he waited with the branding iron, his chiseled face fierce in concentration. He stood well over six feet and filled out his black shirt hard. "Can't say I blame you. Though he looks older than you."

"Yeah. This is actually his spread. He's been Colton's best friend since they were in diapers, and they're only three and a half years older than me. Though it might as well be a million," Dawn murmured.

"Oh. Sorry." In love with her brother's best friend? That did suck.

Dawn shrugged. "I'm of age. I'll graduate from college in a year, and maybe I'll attend graduate school. Someday, he'll be on leave, and he'll see me as an adult. Finally."

"On leave?"

"Hawk's in the Navy, a SEAL. He's on leave for a week and then he goes back. But," she said, sadness creeping into the young woman's words, "it seems like every time he returns home, he's even further away." She was quiet for a moment before perking up. "Though Jake was like that, too, and then he got over it."

"Jake was a SEAL?" Sophie asked.

Dawn shook her head. "No. Army Ranger. I don't know what he did, but I think it took a toll." A wry smile lit her face. "Though he's all better now." A thoughtfulness softened her pretty features. "Not so sure about Quinn."

"Quinn?" Sophie asked.

"Yeah. He was Special Forces—and he doesn't like to talk about it much. He came back and is the sheriff now."

It was nice to get the lowdown from somebody so open and honest. "Your brother's the sheriff?" Sophie asked.

"Yep. Believe me, if it wasn't bad enough trying to find a date with three older brothers, having one of them become the law in town really makes it tough."

Sophie shook her head. "I can imagine." What would it be like to have family that actually cared? That wanted to be involved in your life? The Lodge-Freeze clan intrigued her. "What about Colton? Is he in the service?"

"Nope. He's on spring break. He'll graduate next month with a doctorate in finance. He runs all our family businesses now, but we won't give him the title or salary until he finishes school and then studies international finance abroad for a year or so." Dawn kicked dirt off her boot. "It's a family joke."

Probably had to be clan to understand it. "The family business is the ranch?" Sophie asked.

Dawn shrugged. "The ranches are included in the holdings. We've diversified over the years."

Sounded impressive. Sophie eyed the cowboys. There was a lot more to the Lodge men than she'd thought. "What about you, Dawn? Are you studying finance as well?"

"I'm double majoring in business and photography." The woman teetered on her boots. "The photography is just a hobby, but I do have fun with it."

A hush came over the crowd, and several more people moved toward the fence.

"Buttercup's next," Dawn whispered.

Sophies gaze was riveted on Jake. "Buttercup?"

"Yeah," Dawn confirmed, amusement echoing in her voice. "Jake named him a few years back after the monster connected with a horn."

"Was Jake hurt?" Sophie asked.

Dawn shrugged. "He needed stitches, but it didn't slow him down any." Her gaze stayed on the opened gate to Hawk's left as cowboys prodded the steer inside the pen. The gate slammed shut, and the beast sauntered into the pen.

Sophie lost her breath.

CHAPTER 6

*T*wo sharp, massive horns perched on the largest animal head Sophie had ever seen, ominous and intimidating. Gray fur covered a gigantic body that had to be at least twice the size of the last steer, and its black eyes shone with a devil's light. The animal pawed the ground and huffed, his enormous head swiveling to challenge Jake.

Jake leaned casually against the side fence. "Hi, Buttercup," he said to the amusement of the watching crowd.

Buttercup flicked his tail. His muscles bunched as he snorted again.

"Ready for the timer, Jake?" an older man, his face hidden by the brim of a brown cowboy hat, shouted from the far side of the pen.

Jake looked to Colton and Hawk, who both nodded. "Start the timer."

Fast as a whip and just as unforgiving, Jake struck. His leather glove covered hands latched onto those deadly horns. Buttercup blew out a snort and tossed his head. Jake slid to the side, his face set in brutal concentration, his hands holding tight. A roar rose from the crowd as the steer bucked both feet toward Colton while frantically trying to shake off Jake.

Jake's head jerked back.

With a burst of speed, he pivoted and thrust a muscled thigh into the steer's side. His foot swept the animal's hind legs before he threw all of his weight back, his arms twisting.

Dust swirled around the two.

Buttercup bellowed, legs pawing the ground, before throwing his enormous bulk toward Jake. Grinning fiercely, Jake dodged to the side, barely avoided being crushed, and let the steer's momentum propel them to *thud* against the hard earth.

So fast he was almost a blur, Jake rolled to his side and wedged one knee against the steer's neck, his hands pressing the horns to the ground. The beast fought to regain its feet. Both man and beast panted furiously as dirt drifted around them.

"Sorry, Buttercup, I win today," Jake said softly to the animal.

A round of laughter rose around the pen.

"Whose steer is he?" Sophie released the breath she had been holding, ignoring the buzzing in her ears and the tightness in her belly.

"He's ours," Dawn said.

"Are the rest of the steers owned by the tribe?" Sophie asked.

Dawn shook her head. "Some are owned by tribal members, some by other ranchers in the area. The entire Maverick County gets together once or twice a year to inoculate the animals. Plus"—she jumped down from her perch and sent dust flying—"it's a good reason for a party." She peered up at Sophie. "I'm going to meet some friends by the picnic tables. Do you want to come?"

"No thanks." Sophie smiled down at her. "I'll stay here."

"Don't blame you. There's nothing like a man in chaps, is there?" Dawn headed off.

Sophie turned back to the pen where sharp green eyes

followed Dawn's movements. Hmm. Maybe Hawk wasn't as oblivious as Dawn thought. And the woman was right. There was nothing like a man in chaps.

A tall figure took Dawn's place at Sophie's side. "How are my boys doing?" A deep voice rumbled the question as one scuffed brown boot perched on the bottom railing and two broad arms rested on the top fence slat.

"Your boys?" Sophie glanced into eyes the exact shade of Dawn's.

"Yes. Those two…" He nodded to Jake and Colton. "And that one's close enough—his mama died way too young." He inclined his head toward Hawk. "I'm Tom." He held out a sun-tanned hand.

"Sophie." She appreciated the gentle touch in the large, calloused hand enclosing hers. "They're doing well." She met him eye-to-eye from her position on the higher rung. Thick gray hair was cut short under a brown Stetson, a prominent jaw claimed a rugged stubbornness, and dark Wrangler jeans showed a man still fit and ready to ride. Competency and kindness swirled around him like leaves around a solid oak. Her chest tightened at Tom's words. He considered Jake his son. Roger had always referred to her as "June's daughter, Sophia."

"Oh man, did I miss Buttercup?" Tom glanced toward the far field.

Sophie shook off old memories and laughed. "Yeah, a few minutes ago."

"Darn it. Who won the bet?" Tom asked.

"What bet?"

Tom looked around as if for answers. "On how long it took Jake to take him down."

"I don't know," Sophie admitted.

Tom shrugged. "I would've heard if I won. How was your date with my son?"

"It wasn't a date," Sophie protested as Colton wrestled with the newest steer while Jake remained ready on the sidelines.

"Pity," Tom murmured. "It's about time that boy had some fun."

Sophie nodded toward a grinning Jake. White teeth were illuminated against trails of dirt and sweat. "He's having fun now."

"He sure is," Tom agreed. "I meant the other kind. I thought he might finally be moving on."

"Moving on?" It wasn't any of her business, but...

Tom sighed before answering. "After Emily died, well, we wondered if he'd ever smile again. But he had Leila to worry about."

"He mentioned his wife died young," Sophie said.

"Too young. Way too young to learn what matters in this life." Soberness mellowed Tom's words as Colton jumped back from a newly released steer.

Curiosity clamored through her, and she gave into it. "What matters in life?" Sophie asked.

"Hawk, to your left," Tom called out, tensing until the young man shifted away from kicking hoofs. He returned to their conversation. "You know, what's important. People. Memories. Family." Tom focused over the fence and acknowledged Jake's nod with a nod of his own. He turned toward Sophie and extended an arm. "That was the high sign from Jake. Why don't I escort you over to the picnic tables? He'll be along shortly." All around them people stepped back from the fence, though most kept their attention on the pen.

"High sign?" She took his proffered arm and jumped from her perch.

Tom chortled. "The next three steers are known kickers. Tulip always goes for the crowd."

"Tulip?" Sophie chuckled.

"Yep. Tulip, Snuggles, and Lola. The boys have a sense of humor."

Sophie shook her head as she allowed Tom to escort her across the road to the picnic tables. The walk took some time since they stopped to chat with people along the way. Most folks had heard of her, some asked about her date, and all seemed to like Tom.

Bright red, yellow, and blue-checked cloths covered massive tables where people dug in to delicious-smelling chicken, steak, and sweet fruit salad. Children ran around gleefully while elderly women patted babies and people chatted. Several were obviously of native descent, but just as many people were blond with blue eyes. The whole county must have been in attendance.

"Here we are," Tom said as they arrived at a table where a petite Native American woman uncovered plastic containers. "This is my wife, Loni." Pride filled his words.

"Hi." Sophie released Tom's arm to extend a hand to the pretty woman. Jake's eyes gleamed from a tanned oval face with delicate features and a genuine smile.

"It's nice to meet you, Sophie." Loni smiled and shook her hand. "Please sit. The boys should be along shortly."

Sophie sat and studied Jake's mother. Intelligence that matched Jake's glimmered in her eyes. Sophie took a sip of the sweet, tart lemonade she offered, realizing how thirsty she'd become. "Thank you."

"Sure. So what did you think of the branding? Did you see Buttercup?" Loni asked.

"Yes. Very impressive," Sophie said.

"I heard Quinn won the bet," Loni informed her husband.

Tom rubbed his chin. "Again? Man, that boy has a second sense about that stuff. Unless..."

Loni shook her head. "He and Jake are not in cahoots, Tom. Give it up."

"I don't know." Tom tugged his wife's braid before pecking her cheek with a kiss.

Sophie marveled at the couple's closeness. Her mother and Roger had never seemed to actually like each other. Well, the few times she saw them together, anyway.

"Hey, Mom." Quinn moved into sight, carrying a little girl snuggling her face into his neck. "We have crocodile tears here."

"Tears?" Loni reached up as Quinn transferred a small girl into her waiting arms. "What's wrong, Leila?"

A feminine sniff came from the small child. She lifted her head. "Tommy McAlister pulled my braids and the sheriff won't shoot him."

"Oh." Loni stifled a laugh. "I'm pretty sure the sheriff isn't supposed to shoot people, even if he is your uncle. So, your braids, huh?"

Sniff. "Yeah."

Loni snuggled her closer. "Did it hurt?"

"Well, no…" the girl said.

"But it hurt your feelers?" Loni asked.

"Kind of." Another sniff.

Loni patted Leila's braids. "Now honey, remember when we talked about boys not being quite as smart as girls?"

Twin *hey*s of protest came from Tom and Quinn, as Jake's brother slid onto the bench next to Sophie.

Leila giggled and nodded.

"Okay. Well, they don't know how to talk about important stuff like feelings, so they do stupid stuff instead." Loni winked at Sophie. "Tommy probably just wanted your attention, and that was the only way he could think of to get it."

"Boys are stupid." Leila turned twin dark eyes on Sophie. "Hi."

Sophie smiled at the little girl. She was going to be an incredible beauty one day.

"You're the golf course lady. You went on a date with Daddy," the girl said.

"Ah, no, it, ah, wasn't a date," Sophie sputtered. Quinn coughed back a laugh, and if she had known him better, she'd have elbowed him in the ribs. She settled for giving him a small glare.

Leila's shrewd black gaze met hers across the table. "Did you go on a picnic?"

"Well, yes." Sophie fought to keep from fidgeting under the scrutiny.

"Did you have a pretty view?" Leila asked.

Where was the child going with this? "Definitely."

"And you ate lunch with some wine?" Leila continued.

Sophie's face heated. "Well, yes."

"Sounds like a date to me." Leila clapped her hands in triumph.

Quinn didn't even try to mask his laugh this time.

"Here, Leila, why don't you color for a while?" Loni pushed crayons and a coloring book in front of her granddaughter, causing a blue pencil to roll to the ground.

"I can reach it." Leila leaned down and grabbed the pencil before emitting a soft gasp. "I like your boots." She peeked her little face above the table and stared at Sophie.

There was no way Sophie would admit they were a gift from the girl's father. "Thank you."

"Do you have Manolos?" Leila asked.

Unease pricked Sophie's skin. "I do actually have a pair. They were a gift from my mother for my eighteenth birthday." She had wanted an art easel.

"Oh, are they pretty?" Leila breathed out in longing.

"Um, yeah. Pink and sparkly." Sophie smiled.

A frown marred Leila's pretty face. "I wish I could see them."

"Well." Sophie reached for a blank piece of paper and the pink pencil. "Let's see what we can do about that." Her hand moved with sure strokes as she drew the shoes. Leila watched intently until Sophie handed over the paper.

Leila held the paper as if it were infinitely precious. "Wow, they are pretty." She stared at the delicate sandals dangling from a pine tree. "Is this for me?"

"It's all yours," Sophie confirmed.

"Sophie, you are so talented," Loni noted in admiration just as a shadow crossed the table.

Pleasure tipped through Sophie. Although these people were all strangers, she felt comfortable. Accepted. She marveled at the little girl surrounded by such love and protection.

"What's that?" Jake asked from behind her. Sophie's heartbeat increased.

"My Manolos, Daddy." Leila's excitement made the effort seem much more than it was. "See?" She held out the paper to her father, who took it over Sophie's shoulder.

"Wow. They are pretty." Jake handed the drawing back to his daughter. "My mother's right—you are very talented." He settled onto the bench next to her, effectively trapping her between two hard male bodies. Talk about immovable objects.

His compliment had her feeling like she'd aced a difficult test. Gaining control over her emotions, she glanced at the lawyer. "You showered."

Jake nodded. "In the bunkhouse. Believe me, it was necessary." Clean jeans hung low on tight hips over black boots while a light black shirt emphasized the corded strength in his upper body. His wet hair curled over his collar. For once, the dark strands weren't tied back, and the thick mass lent him a dangerous air.

Almost primitive.

JAKE SETTLED onto the picnic bench, his attention on the woman who had fit so nicely into his family gathering. Though her pretty picture of city shoes should have brought him back to reality. Like being dosed with freezing water. Except cold wasn't something he equated with Sophie. Pure heat. Full sunshine. Raging fire. He wanted nothing more than to jump into the flames and get burned. His cock flared to life behind his zipper, and he fought a groan. Now wasn't the time.

Quinn sent him a smart-assed look over Sophie's head.

Damn younger brother had always been a mind reader. Jake scowled back.

Colton loped up and settled into the seat across the table. He'd showered and stolen one of Jake's shirts to wear. The guy was a genius with money, but he couldn't remember to bring a complete change of clothing. "Let's eat. I'm starving," he said. He flipped open a lid covering freshly prepared fried chicken as Loni passed plates all around. Different salads and cookies completed the meal.

Sophie nibbled on a drumstick, and Jake fought another groan. Those pretty lips were much too talented to be wasted on chicken.

Colton glanced around. "Where's Dawnie?"

"She went to eat down by the pond with a bunch of friends." Tom scooped more pieces of watermelon onto Leila's plate.

"What friends?" Colton handed Leila the napkin she'd dropped.

Loni shrugged. "I just saw her with Adam." She handed the bowl of chicken over to Colt.

"Adam?" Quinn shook his head. "I don't like her singing in that band with him."

"Me, neither." Jake bit his lip. Maybe it was time to intervene and pull Dawn from the band. She didn't belong in a bar.

Sophie put her napkin on her empty plate. "Dawn's in a band?"

"Yes. The gal sings like an angel." Tom's chest puffed out.

"She should be singing in church, not with Adam," Quinn muttered.

Loni rolled her eyes. "Adam is Hawk's best friend, Quinn. He's as *safe* as they get."

"Adam is anything but safe, Mom," Quinn countered.

Loni shook her head. "Leave Dawn alone, all of you. She has to find her own way, and you three"—she peered at her husband —"I mean, you *four*, are going to do nothing but push her in the wrong direction. Trust me."

Colton opened his mouth to respond and then jumped as a small hand slapped him on the back.

"Nice job with the steers, Colt," a curvy brunette said, smiling. "Hi Loni, Tom."

"Hi, Melanie." Loni introduced the young woman to Sophie. "Have you eaten?"

Melanie nodded to Sophie and smiled. "Yes, ma'am, and it's nice to meet you, Sophie. I'm just heading down to watch Jonsie ride a bronc in the left pasture."

"Count me in." Colton jumped to his feet and slung an arm around Melanie. "See you later, Mom." He pulled the woman away.

"They make a nice couple," Sophie noted with a pretty smile.

Loni watched them go. "They've been the best of buddies since preschool. Though," she said, her eyes twinkling with mischief, "I can't wait until he looks up one day and realizes she's all grown up."

"Boys are stupid," Leila muttered.

Her grandmother nodded.

CHAPTER 7

onday morning, Sophie found herself in the middle of her pretty room with the golf course design calling from the desk and her sketchbook beckoning from her bed. She had work to do, but she wanted to draw the scene of Colton chasing a steer. She had spent half the night capturing Jake wrestling Buttercup to the ground. It was her best work.

The shrill of an antique pink phone saved her from having to make a decision, and she jumped across the bed to answer it. She stretched out on her belly before saying hello.

A soft country ballad wafted through the line. "Hi there, Sophie, I hope I'm not phoning too early."

"Hi, Loni, no, I'm just getting to work." Well, she'd been thinking about getting to work, anyway.

"Oh, good. That's why I wanted to call you. I'd like to hire you. Well, I mean, that we would like to hire you. The tribal council, that is," Loni said.

Sophie sat up. "Hire me? For what?"

"We finally have enough funds to build a garden in memory of a good friend of mine. We want it near the base of headquarters, close to Spades Mountain, you know, the one with all the hiking and horse trails?" Loni asked.

Sophie had no idea. "What do you need from me?"

"We need you to design it. You have a landscape design degree, right?"

A garden? Sophie's breath caught. "Well, yes. But I specialize in golf courses." Though it would be interesting to design a garden—and probably be good for her résumé. Just in case.

"But your public hearing isn't for another week and your designs are all finished, aren't they?" Loni asked.

Sophie's heartbeat quickened as her mind spun with creative ideas. "Yes."

"Then this might be fun. Plus, you'd be working with the council, so you'd have time to sell everyone on the golf course." Loni's voice turned even more chipper.

"You dangle quite the carrot, Loni," Sophie said, laughing.

"Yeah, it's a gift. We'd pay you for the garden design."

The project sounded interesting, and branching out to another type of design appealed to the artist inside Sophie. "I don't know…"

"Tell you what. The council is meeting for lunch today. Why don't I schedule the first fifteen minutes for you to present your golf course design, and then you can stay and listen to our plans. Plus, Mrs. Shiller has bridge today, so you'd be eating all alone. What fun is that?" Loni asked.

What a kind invitation. "All right." Plus, Sophie needed to take every opportunity to convince people her designs worked. "I'll be there. Tribal Headquarters at eleven?"

"Yes. See you then." Loni ended the call. Probably before Sophie could change her mind.

❧   ❧   ❧

A COUPLE of hours after the phone call with Loni, Sophie drove the hill toward headquarters, her new boots working the pedals of the Jeep. She told herself that she'd taken extra care with her makeup to prepare for a business meeting and not because Jake may be at headquarters.

Then she told herself to stop lying—it wasn't healthy.

Loni met her at the door and took one of the large, mounted designs to help carry inside. They headed into the familiar conference room and placed the designs on easels. Loni then introduced Sophie to three men, appearing to range in age from sixty to ninety, named Earl, Jacob, and Freddie, along with two silver-haired women, June and Phyllis, whom she'd already met at the picnic.

"The chief may pop in, and Jake should be here sometime." Loni gestured for Sophie to grab a plate and sandwich from the table.

Sophie did so and sat beside Freddie, whose smile took up his entire face. "Jake is on the council?" she asked.

"No. But we act much like a Board of Directors, and every board needs a lawyer." Loni sat on Sophie's other side and selected a turkey sandwich.

Freddie pushed his plate away. His long jowls swung as he spoke, and his deep brown eyes surveyed a platter of cookies with interest. He carefully selected one. "I hear the sheriff won the pot again this year."

"Quinn has a knack for that kind of thing." Loni protested, her eyes gleaming. "Those boys are not in cahoots."

"Humph," Freddie replied around the cookie.

Sophie dropped her napkin on her empty plate. "What was the pot, anyway?"

"About two grand this year." Freddy rubbed his chin.

Sophie swung her gaze to him. "Two thousand dollars?"

Loni shrugged. "It's an event. Every year." She sat back. "All right, Sophie, show us your plan." She nodded toward the colorful renderings.

Drawing in a breath, Sophie stood and passed out packets detailing the project that had residences scattered every two acres. "The group is proposing a golf course community, most likely for retirement folks, with a clubhouse and restaurant. It's close enough to Maverick that the public could come golf for the day, maybe on the way to the tribe's casino, three miles down the road." She paused and walked to the renderings. "The Charleton Group has developed similar properties all over the world with great success."

"Didn't the Group buy this property with a development in mind?" Phyllis asked, her face buried in the papers.

Sophie tightened her knees to halt their trembling. "I believe so, yes."

"That was gutsy since the county commissioners could refuse their permit," Freddie chimed in.

Sophie nodded. "The Group seems confident the law will allow the development. Their lawyers are more up to date with the legal aspects of the proposal than I am. My area of focus is the golf course design."

"This does look like a fun course," June mused, her large, round eyes magnified by thick glasses. "Check out those sand traps around the fifth green."

Jacob nodded. "And the water hazard on the sixteenth hole. Man, that'd be fun."

Loni's eyes lit up. "This is a wonderful design, Sophie. I like how the residential lots are two entire acres while keeping the feel of the country. The council meets again tomorrow, and we'll discuss an official position on your proposal."

The council had been more receptive than Sophie had hoped. Her shoulders slowly relaxed. "Thank you." She retook her seat.

"Our next item on the agenda is Willa's Garden at the base of the road." Loni perched narrow glasses on her nose.

Sophie took a sip of her sparkling water.

Loni turned toward Sophie. "Willa served on the council until she became too ill and passed away. She taught school for thirty years before that and never married. The tribe was her family."

"So was the entire community, tribal or not," June spoke up.

The loving way the board spoke about Willa touched Sophie. Ideas shot through her head. A community garden? "How much land are we talking? Do you want fields for sports?"

Loni shook her head. "No. In fact, we're going to build an entire sports complex on the other side of the high school. That could be your next project. For Willa's Garden, we just want peace and tranquility."

Sophie's hands itched to get ahold of her charcoals and start designing, but she'd never planned a large scale garden. "I can draft up a design for you and then see what you think."

"By Wednesday?" June's face brightened.

Sophie tried to contain her own excitement. "I can have a rough design by then."

"Excellent." Earl leaped to his feet. "Come on guys, bingo starts in an hour at the casino." The other two men tossed their empty plates into the trash and followed him out the door.

"Thanks again, Sophie," Freddie called over his shoulder.

Sophie smiled. They'd drawn her in as if she were one of them. Being included shouldn't matter to her. Yet she couldn't lose the smile. She stood and expected handshakes, but both ladies gave her gentle hugs on their way out the door. Clearing her throat, she moved to help Loni clear the rest of the table.

A deep voice from the doorway startled her. "Drop those sandwiches, Mom." Jake strode in, his eyes focused on the food as his mother handed him a plate.

Sophie had found the man devastating in chaps. That was

nothing compared to his look in full charcoal-gray Armani. The dark silk outlined his strength, while his red tie radiated power. The subtle stripe in his pants emphasized the impressive length of his legs. Butterflies danced in her stomach.

She lived in a big city. Muscles were achieved in gyms and exercise rooms. Jake earned his the hard way—outdoors battling nature, adding a wildness she should resist. Men like him didn't exist in her world, and she didn't fit in with theirs. But those butterflies beat with furious wings and didn't give a hoot about logic. Or safety.

She needed to shut her mouth before she drooled.

His dimple winked and his gaze ran over her face like a kid eyeing licorice in a candy store.

Her gaze dropped to his lips. She remembered how his mouth felt against hers, his tongue tangling with hers, and she flushed. His lips curved in response.

"How was court, dear?" Loni pushed the plate of cookies toward her son.

Jake released Sophie's gaze and dropped onto a vacated chair. "Idiot EPA," he mumbled between bites.

Loni tapped the unused napkins into a neat pile. "Jake, are you done working for the day?"

"Definitely," he said.

Loni edged toward the door. "Good. Sophie needs to see the five acres for Willa's Garden, and I have an appointment in town. Would you show it to her?"

"Subtle, Mom. Yes, I'd love to show Sophie around," Jake said.

The double meaning wasn't lost on Sophie. Probably wasn't lost on his mother, either.

"Good. 'Bye." Loni made her escape.

Sophie clasped her suddenly shaking hands. She had the oddest urge to tackle the lawyer to the ground and steal a kiss but busied herself gathering the extra copies of her presentation. What was wrong with her?

"So they suckered you in, huh?" Jake turned amused eyes on her.

Oh yeah. Her job. The one she loved. Man, she lost all sense of reality when Jake was around. She ran a quick hand over her face. "Completely. Easily and without much of an effort." Of course it helped that she wanted to design the garden.

"They do that." Jake grabbed another cookie. "But—" He paused, obviously to choose the right words. "The tribe isn't going to support the Charleton Group's golf course proposal on that land no matter how much we like your design."

Sophie stilled. "Are you sure?" Maybe he was wrong about the council. They seemed to like the proposed development.

Jake rubbed his chin. "They may come across like a sweet, old, bingo-playing group, but they're ruthless. Before you know it, ten years will have passed and you'll have designed everything from memorials to summer gardens. We both know you're meant to be in the city."

She frowned. "We both know I belong in the city?" The man had just met her. At his nod, she raked her gaze over his now relaxed form. "Look who's talking. Armani looks good on you, Jake." She'd bet anything he was a force to watch in a courtroom.

One eyebrow lifted. "I was in court today."

"Obviously. What wrong are you and the EPA trying to right?" she asked.

"Ah, stereotyping, are we?" His narrowed eyes belied his lazy drawl.

Heat roared through her ears. "Excuse me?"

"I sat on the opposite side from the EPA today, sweetheart." He explained why the tribes often sat across the fence from the government.

She tilted her head. Every time she thought she had a handle on Jake Lodge, he surprised her again. His analytical mind complemented his sexy grin in a way that would intrigue any woman, but she had to fight her attraction in order to save her uncle's company.

"Come on, we can load these, and then I'll take you to the memorial site." Jake stood and tossed his trash into the can before grabbing both foam boards with the golf course designs and holding out a hand.

She relaxed and placed her hand in Jake's much larger one. Warmth shot heat to her lower stomach. Warmth she didn't want to feel.

Because he was right. She was a city girl.

Wasn't she?

CHAPTER 8

The memorial site had been beautiful. Hours after surveying it with Jake, and back at the B&B, Sophie sketched a quick garden design including natural stone paths, a koi pond, and picnic areas.

The site had been perfect for the memorial, and she'd enjoyed tromping through the brush with Jake after he'd thrown on cowboy boots. Even in a suit, the man looked natural surrounded by wild nature. He hadn't tried to kiss her again, and she told herself she was glad. There was no future for them.

Although that hadn't stopped her from agreeing to dinner with his family. She glanced at the clock. He'd return for her in less than an hour.

The cell phone jarred her out of her musings.

"Hi, Sophia." Preston's voice came smooth and sure over the line. "Miss me?"

Not so much, actually. *Interesting.* "I've been working. How's the Seattle job going?" she asked, instead of answering his question.

"Don't ask. We've run into some interesting competition. How's it going with the tribe?" Preston asked.

Her shoulders hunched. "I'm not sure. They all like the design but don't want it on the Charleton Group's land."

He rustled papers over the line. "They're still objecting?"

"We may not have tribal support when we face the county commissioners next week." Dread chilled her gut.

"The Group's lawyers are pretty good. You'll just describe your design, and they'll offer the proposal for the permit," Preston said.

Thank goodness she had backup at the hearing.

Preston cleared his throat before speaking again. "I've done a bit of research. You haven't run across Jake Lodge, have you?"

The air caught in her lungs. She took several deep breaths. "I've met Lodge. He's the tribe's lawyer." And the man who had kissed her into oblivion. "Why?"

"He's good. Really good. Took on the state twice, won both times in the U.S. Supreme Court. Tell me he's not involved in opposing the project," Preston said.

Sophie coughed. "I'd say he is involved. Very. Though he hasn't seemed too fired up about opposing us."

"Probably the calm before he strikes. I've heard he's the shark of all sharks. Plus, there are rumors that the tribe wants to build its own golf course over by the casino and are out to prevent any competition."

"No, you've got it wrong," her voice came out firmer than she intended. "Jake's not like that."

Quiet echoed across the line. "Just how well do you know him?" Preston asked.

"I've met with him regarding the proposal." Heat slid into her face.

Preston cleared his throat. "Of course. Well, I guess I'd just tell you to watch your back."

She needed to get off the phone. Now. "No problem."

"Have you given any thought to taking the cruise with me?" Preston asked.

No. Not at all. She'd been too busy mooning over a danger-ous, country badass of a lawyer who might just torpedo her proposal. "The cruise? I, ah, don't know. I should probably concentrate on work right now. We need to save Uncle Nathan's company." She didn't want to hurt Preston's feelings. He was a good man. On paper, they so worked. In reality? Maybe not.

"I'm not taking no for an answer. Keep thinking about it. 'Bye." He ended the call.

Sophie set her phone down and stared sightlessly at the drawings before her. Just a week ago she would've jumped at the chance for a cruise with Preston. Now she balked. Why? She reached for her sketchbook and flipped it open to the second page. The answer stared back at her with Jake's eyes.

What was she thinking, agreeing to a dinner at the Lodge house? Jake stirred feelings in her that all but guaranteed a broken heart when she left—when she returned home.

Why did home seem so far away?

Hurriedly, she changed and then headed downstairs. She waited for Jake on the wooden porch swing, her nervous motions swaying the comfortable seat back and forth.

The thud of thick boots on the wide steps announced his arrival.

"No Armani tonight, Jake?" Sophie raised an eyebrow at his dark patterned button-up shirt, faded jeans, and polished cowboy boots. Combined with the deep black eyes, rugged face, and jet hair curling over his collar, he all but screamed bad-boy handsome. A true temptation for some girl to try and tame.

Some *country girl* to try and tame.

"You look spring pretty." His tone was pure sin.

Electricity zinged through her when she took his proffered hand and walked to the truck with him. "I think your family is matchmaking." It wasn't what she'd meant to say.

"They like you." He stopped her at the black truck, pressing her against the hard metal. "So do I." He lowered his head, giving her all the time in the world to resist or shift away.

She didn't move. Her breath caught with anticipation.

Warm and soft, his lips wandered over hers before he deepened the kiss to something intimate, something demanding. Sophie sighed deep in her throat. One broad hand molded itself to her lower back and pulled her against him. Sheer masculine strength met her softness.

Her heart pounded, and need thrummed between her legs. Her nipples peaked to sharp points. Fire lashed through her nerves—fire for him.

Jake raised his head, his face an inch from hers, his eyes the dark clouds of a summer storm. "You have a decision to make."

"What?" Confusion battled with the desire ripping through her veins.

"There's something here." He dropped a gentle kiss to her lips. "I want to explore it."

"Jake—"

Broad, warm hands skimmed down her arms. "I'm not asking for forever. We both know our lives exist in different worlds. But we're here now. For a brief time," he said.

She fought a shiver. It was tempting. To lose herself in all that strength. The pure maleness of the man. "I'll think about it."

His triumphant expression made her question her sanity. She barely knew him, for goodness sake. He released her and opened his door. She scrambled over the seat and secured her seat belt. He gracefully sat and ignited the engine, driving away from the B&B. "How's the garden design going?" he asked once they were on the way.

She shook her head to concentrate. A dangerous ache pounded through her body, blooming at the apex of her legs. "The garden? Great. Mrs. Shiller helped with possible placement of flowers and shrubs."

"It's very nice of you to include her," Jake said, speeding out of town toward the surrounding mountains. "Are you seeing anyone?"

Sophie jumped at the unexpected question. "No." An invitation to a cruise didn't count.

"Me neither." Jake's tone carried a hint of something unreadable.

"I said I'd think about it," she said. Jake Lodge was becoming too much of a temptation. Her body pressed her to say yes. Her mind reeled for her to stay grounded. She turned and admired the changing landscape, searching for a safe topic of conversation. "Rumor has it Quinn won the Buttercup pot the last couple of years." She sent a sly glance Jake's way.

Jake grinned. "Yeah, Quinn has a knack for it, I guess."

"You're not in cahoots?" she asked.

"No." It was Jake's turn to glance sideways. "But...you won't tell anyone?"

For once, she could be in on the joke. "I promise."

Jake lifted one shoulder in a tough-guy shrug. "Quinn has a formula."

"Your brother has a formula?"

Jake nodded. "Quinn takes last years' time, subtracts two seconds for Buttercup's aging a year, and then multiplies it by a factor of how many injuries I'd sustained the past year."

"Really?"

"Yep. He's won the last four years in a row." Jake's deep chuckle sent a skittering along her nerve endings.

Injuries? Wait a minute. "Do you get injured a lot in court?" She couldn't help teasing him.

He turned a steep corner, his hands relaxed on the wheel. "Not usually in court. I work my ranch, and injuries are common. But my brothers and I have the routine down, so we're fairly safe."

Longing flowed through her as she realized she'd missed out

on something important by being an only child. "You and your brothers seem really close."

"We are. If for no other reason than to keep Dawnie safe. That woman's a menace. The second she started noticing boys, one in particular, life changed for all of us," Jake shook his head as the truck splashed through a couple of mud-puddles.

"Hawk seems like a decent guy." A group of horses caught her attention, their manes waving a myriad of colors through the wind as they galloped over hills.

Jake flashed her a surprised glance. "He's way too old for her. And a dead man if he goes near her. Besides, his job's screwing him up as bad as—" Jake's jaw snapped shut.

"Screwing him up as bad as the Rangers did you?" Would he let her in? Actually let her know him? The desire for his trust caught Sophie unaware.

"Who've you been talking to?" His attention was riveted completely on her.

Man, he probably nailed witnesses on cross-examination. "Nobody." Sophie struggled not to squirm.

Jake turned his focus to the road. "I've made my peace with the things we did in the service. And no," he noted as she leaned forward to speak, "I won't tell you about it right now."

"Oh." She sat back, way too much pleasure coursing through her at the idea that they had more than *right now*. "Were you married while in the army?"

"No. I married Em one month after my discharge." He frowned. "She was too young. Wanted a big life in the big city. I just wanted a normal life. After the service." He turned the truck through the massive logs standing vigil at the foot of a spectacular ranch. "We dated in high school and ran into each other my first night back. I hadn't even seen my parents yet. Tequila led to bourbon, and one thing led to another. We found out she was pregnant three weeks later." He shook his head. "Leila is the biggest blessing of my life, but I wish things had been different for Emily."

"How did she die?" Sophie kept her voice low. He was trusting in her, whether he knew it or not.

Jake's eyes went flat. "I'm not sure what happened. I knew she was unhappy here, but it could've been postpartum. It was the dead of winter and I was back east arguing a case. She asked my mom to watch the baby, packed her bags into a little two-seater sports car I'd bought her during the summer, and headed out. In a blizzard. In a summer car." His voice turned hoarse. "She ran off the road and down an incline. Doc said she was dead on impact—that she didn't suffer."

Sophie's heart clenched. "I'm so sorry, Jake." She ran a hand along his tense arm, and the muscles rippled at her touch.

Jake nodded. Then he stopped the truck in a circular drive of a two-story log home and turned toward her. "Enough bad memories. We're supposed to have fun tonight." His knuckle brushed her cheekbone. "And you're supposed to be deciding to sleep with me."

CHAPTER 9

*T*om saved Sophie from having to reply when he hurried out a massive double-wooden door and opened her truck door. She accepted his hand, and he helped her to the ground. Sophie smiled at her savior and turned to admire the large, custom log home. A wide, gleaming wood porch ran the length of the front and invited people to sit on swings or comfortable-looking chairs.

"Sophie, we're so glad you could make it." Tom gently took her elbow and led her up the porch and into the warm interior of a wide entryway. The smell of apple pie filled the air while soft country music floated throughout.

Directly ahead, floor-to-ceiling windows showcased Mineral Lake and the surrounding mountains. A massive stone fireplace took up one wall while beautiful Western oils filled the other. Sophie took a moment to admire the deep colors of a Gollings painting of barely tamed horses stamping the snow near a jagged mountain, and then she swept her gaze around the rest of the room.

Leather couches and hand-carved wooden tables sat comfortably on a thick Native American style rug. Several coloring books and a smattering of crayons scattered across the largest table, and the smell of leather and pine mixed with the apple pie scent.

A delighted feminine shriek made Sophie jump when Leila flew into her with Colton on her heels.

"Help, Sophie, help me." Leila shielded herself behind Sophie's body, her tiny hands tight on Sophie's waist.

"She can't protect you," Colton growled out in a low, monster-like voice.

"Yes, she can." Leila poked her head around to stick her tongue out at her uncle. "I'll tell the sheriff on you, Uncle Colt."

Colton grabbed for her just as she dodged to the other side of Sophie, who struggled to keep her balance. "Then I'll have to tickle both the sheriff and you, squirt."

"Don't let him get me." Leila giggled from behind her.

"I'm pretty sure we can take him, Leila," Sophie said solemnly, trying not to laugh.

The game ended when Jake yanked his daughter into the air to smack noisy kisses along her face. "Is Colton picking on you, precious?" He kicked the front door shut.

"Yes, Daddy." Leila giggled again. "Beat him up."

Jake swung her onto his back. "Ah, Leila, it's just too easy. A man my age needs a challenge."

"A man your age needs a walker," his brother retorted. Then he turned vibrant blue eyes on her, reaching in. "Hi, Soph."

His easy hug brought a lump to her throat. They were just like the families she used to watch on television.

"Oh, hello, Sophie." Loni walked in from the left, wiping her hands on a dishtowel. "Come give me a hand in the kitchen, would you?" She nodded to the men. "The salmon isn't going to barbecue itself, boys."

Sophie watched as the men headed through the kitchen and gathered around a humongous silver barbecue on the outside deck with Leila still perched on her father's shoulders.

"What can I do?" Sophie glanced around. Chopped vegetables sat on a large cutting board near a deep red bowl.

"Sit at the bar and keep me company." Loni nodded toward thick brown barstools on the other side of the spotless silver granite countertop. Sophie took a seat while Loni poured them both a glass of wine.

"How are the garden designs coming?" Loni asked while resuming her chopping.

Sophie took a sip. The buttery chardonnay tasted of smooth sweetness. "Great. I should have something concrete for you by tomorrow's meeting."

Loni sobered. "I'm so glad. Also, the council met, and we all really like your golf course design."

"But?" Sophie steeled herself for the news.

Loni waved one hand in the air. "We don't like it in that location. We've put out some feelers for alternate places. Sorry."

They were rejecting Sophie's design and not her, but her stomach rolled. "I was afraid of that. Jake already warned me the council wouldn't support the project."

"Really?" Loni raised an eyebrow.

"That's the only property the Charleton Group owns, and they're pretty determined to develop it." There *had* to be a way to convince the tribe to back the design. What if her uncle lost his business? Failure tasted like ashes.

"Well, the county commissioner meeting should be interesting, then." Loni scraped the veggies into the bowl. "Let's head out to the deck."

Sophie took a deep breath. She'd enjoy dinner with a nice family, and then go back to her room and figure out another angle. Her proposal could still be accepted by the county without the tribe's backing.

She grabbed the other salad sitting on the counter, followed Loni to the deck, and settled into a cushioned chair between Jake and Leila at the round glass patio table. The sun set to the west, spreading fingers of pink and orange across the sky. Colton sat across from her, and the withdrawing sun highlighted the myriad of colors in his hair. She should've brought her oil paints.

They all dug into the fish and salad, and Loni passed homemade rolls around that smelled better than anything found in the city. After a short time, Sophie relaxed and started to enjoy the excellent meal.

The casual teasing between Jake and Colton made her laugh. Their easy camaraderie was something she'd missed, being an only child. Both brothers stilled when she asked about Dawn's absence. Apparently the girl was on a date. Maybe having older brothers had its drawbacks.

"Who is she out with?" Sophie took another sip of wine after Tom topped off her glass.

"Some college senior." Colton said the word *college* like an expletive.

Tom nodded. "She's just out with Frankston to make Hawk jealous."

"Hawk's too old for her." Jake reached over to tug his daughter's ear. She squealed and slapped him playfully before digging back into her apple pie.

Loni placed another piece of pie onto Colton's plate. "He's only a few years older."

"I wasn't talking birthdates, Mom." Jake's eyes hardened as he stared at something only he could see.

"He's a good kid." Tom pushed his plate away from himself and groaned. "But Jake's right. He's too old for our girl."

Loni watched as Jake yanked on his daughter's braid again. "Our girl knows her own heart, boys."

"Knock it off, Daddy." Leila grinned around a mouth full of apple pie. "Or I'll tell the sheriff on you."

Colton frowned. "What's up with all this *telling the sheriff* talk, kid? I'm the cool uncle."

"Yeah, but Uncle Quinn has a badge. And a gun." Leila's eyes lit up as Colton sat forward.

"I'm way tougher than the sheriff," Colton said.

"Yeah, but he really loves me, Uncle Colt," Leila said.

Sophie didn't miss the sly grin Jake gave his mother.

"I love you more, baby doll," Colton said.

"Enough to give me that new pony Merriment foaled last month?" The little girl pursed her lips.

Tom guffawed in laughter. "Boy did you walk into that one, son."

"I was thinking the new foal would make a good Christmas present for a really good little girl." Colton raised an eyebrow at Jake, who gave an imperceptible nod.

"I'm really good." Leila widened her eyes to pure adorable innocence.

Colton shook his head. "Hm. I don't know."

"You'd be my favoritest uncle, Colton." The little girl flung herself onto his lap and wrapped tiny arms around a strong neck.

Colton's eyes softened as he gazed at the little minx. "You are going to be one very dangerous woman someday, baby doll."

"Then it'd be good to be my favoritest uncle, wouldn't it?" Leila smacked his cheek with a wet kiss.

"Without question." Colton pecked her on the nose before Leila jumped down, a successful smile on her face as she returned to her seat.

So this was what families could be. Should be. A pang hit Sophie in the solar plexus.

"Speaking of the unfavoritest uncle, where is Quinn?" Colton finished off his pie.

Tom shrugged. "I heard that maybe he was dating someone from Maverick." Tom rolled his eyes at Loni as if she'd put him up to introducing the subject.

"Her name's Juliet, and she tolt Uncle Quinn to take a flying leap," Leila piped up.

"I knew it!" Loni exclaimed, leaning forward. "How do you know that, sweetheart?"

"I axed him." The little girl pushed her plate away. "When me and Uncle Quinn got smoothies at the ice-cream place, Juliet was just leaving. I tolt Uncle that she was pretty and he should take her to the movies, and he said he'd already axed, but she said to take a flying leap." Leila screwed her face into a frown. "He didn't say where he was 'posed to leap to."

"The plot thickens," Colton murmured with a pointed look at his brother.

Jake snorted. "Nah, she somehow got the gist of his sparkling personality."

Sophie shook her head. The family was so involved with one another, whether they all liked it or not.

In too short a time, she sat in Jake's truck next to Leila as they drove her back to the B&B. They both walked her to her door, and she was grateful Jake couldn't press her for an answer to his invitation for wild sex.

She wasn't sure she would say no.

MORNING ARRIVED ALL TOO SOON. Sophie drove the twenty minutes toward Mineral Lake and followed the directions to the headquarters of Concerned Citizens for Rural Development, located about halfway between town and the Kooskia Reservation. The headquarters was housed in a large metal shop with a hard-packed dirt floor lined with wooden benches. A rectangular metal table perched on a one-foot dais in the front of the room, and three matching chairs behind the table faced the crowd. A narrow podium stood over to one side, and a hand-sewn emblem of the planet adorned the wall. The smell of dirt and sweat assaulted her nose.

Her cell phone rang just as she walked inside the cool interior, and she quickly said hello.

"Hi, Sophie. There's a two-hour break in my trial today. Want to do lunch?" Jake asked.

She fought an involuntary smile. "Um, maybe. It depends if I'm done by then."

"Where are you?" he asked.

A woman up front waved, and Sophie started up the aisle toward the tall blonde wearing tan capris and a high-collared white blouse. "Meeting with Concerned Citizens."

"In Mineral Lake?" he asked.

"No. About fifteen miles outside of the town."

Jake's groan sounded irritated somehow. "Not the Concerned Citizens for Rural Development Group."

"One and the same," she said, looking at the rows of seats.

"By yourself?" Jake's voice dropped to a low tone.

Her steps faltered. "Um, yeah."

"Soph." Exasperation lived on his exhale. "Wait to go inside."

"Too late. Have to go, 'bye." She shut the phone and dropped it into her bag before extending her hand to the woman. "I'm Sophie Smith."

"Judy Rockefeller." Classically straight features in a pale, makeup-free face frowned as they shook hands. Her mood was cool and her shake stiff.

Maybe Sophie shouldn't have come alone. "So, where do you want me?" She shook off unease while people filed into the room and took their places on the benches. If the tribe refused to back her design, she needed support from county citizens. She stepped back from Judy.

Judy pointed to the closest metal chair behind the table. "You can sit there. Reverend Moseby will sit next to you, and my husband, Billy, will sit next to him. Billy is our president."

"Okay." Sophie stepped onto the dais and dropped her bag next to the seat. "Do you want me to give a presentation or just answer questions?"

Judy waved at newcomers before turning back to Sophie. "Billy will talk for a bit, and then people will ask you questions. You don't need to describe the proposal. Everyone has already studied the golf course plan from the county's records."

"The records? You mean the application for the conditional-use permit?" Sophie's stomach danced uncomfortably as several people watched her from the audience.

"Yes," Judy said.

A side door opened and two men entered, walking close. The first wore all black with a priest's collar, his belly stretching the dark fabric until streaks of white showed through. Sharp blue eyes rested on Sophie. "Miss Smith, I'm Reverend Moseby." He extended a beefy hand for her to shake, his ruddy face contrasting with his sparse white hair.

Sophie shook his hand and tried not to grimace at his dampened flesh. She unobtrusively wiped her palm on her flowered skirt upon being released.

"I'm Billy Rockefeller." The second man held out a hand and gave Sophie a firm shake. Judy's husband wore his blue jacket with a presidential pin like a Masters champion. His perfect posture hinted at an unyielding spine.

"Hi," Sophie released him to go take her assigned seat.

Billy sat as the reverend approached the podium and opened the meeting with a recap of the previous month's meeting before everyone bowed their heads to pray.

"Please bless this wondrous gathering of these wondrous people out to protect the earth itself." The reverend's voice rose in pitch and volume. "And bless our guest today. Let her see the folly of destroying the God-given earth and all its bounty. Let Christ guide us, his hand firm and deadly if need be. May the might of the Lord fill us, guide us, and pummel those who oppose us."

The group gave a collective amen as Sophie searched for the closest exit, her heart in her throat. Did he say "deadly"? The twangy song from *Deliverance* danced through her head. The reverend turned the podium over to Billy Rockefeller.

Billy stood and crossed to the podium, his black boots ringing loud and strong across the stage. Flak boots with a fancy jacket? Weird.

He rested both hands on the hard wood and waited with a dramatic pause before speaking. "Thanks for coming out today, folks. The first item on the agenda involves the protection of the wolves in the area."

Sophie felt the blood drain from her face when she noticed a handgun tucked casually into Billy's waistband.

He continued. "At this point, the wolves are threatening our livestock—our very livelihood. What do we do to threats like that?"

"Eliminate them," came the collective response.

Surely this wasn't a veiled threat directed toward her.

Billy nodded. "There's a court trial going on regarding the wolves near tribal lands right now. I'll let you know the outcome as soon as I can."

Sophie frowned. She felt safe disagreeing with the tribe; she felt anything but safe sitting like easy prey behind the metal table with this citizen group. What had she gotten herself into? She mentally shook her head. Boy, was her imagination going crazy.

Billy cleared his throat. "The second item on the agenda involves the new development proposal in front of the county commissioners. It includes a golf course. The designer, Sophie Smith, has graciously agreed to answer your questions today." He inclined his head toward Sophie.

She stood, her legs shaky. Was she supposed to go to the podium or just turn around? Not wanting to be too near Billy, she just faced the audience with her back to the wall so she could see everybody.

A sandy blond haired man with a thick goatee raised a hand, and Billy nodded at him. "I'm Fred Gregton. I'm wondering how much human life is worth to your development group?"

Sophie frowned. "I don't understand your question, Mr. Gregton."

"Of course you don't. More traffic on the road from Maverick is going to kill somebody, Miss Smith. I'm just wondering if your development group gives a shit about that," Gregton said.

A couple of people nodded.

"Well..." Sophie leaned forward, her heart beating rapidly. "It's my understanding the traffic study conducted by the developer shows that the road is fine."

"Bullshit." Gregton spat on the floor.

Sophie's temper began to stir among the fear.

Another hand went up, this one belonging to a middle-age woman wearing a denim jumper. "I'd like to know why you're the only one here today. It's my understanding that you are just the designer of the golf course community. Where is the actual developer?"

Sophie floundered for an answer. "Their headquarters is in southern California."

"Will they be attending the hearing in front of the county commissioners?" the woman asked.

Sophie nodded. "I know one of the Group's attorneys will be there, but I haven't heard who else will attend."

"So," Gregton spoke up again as the crowd seemed to get restless, "we're not important enough for them to meet with."

"They sent me, Mr. Gregton." Just how out-of-hand would

this crazy group get? It was apparent most of them were armed. Why were so many guns needed just for an informational meeting? Sophie's gaze flew to the door at the sound of hoofbeats outside. Great. More people to add to the tension.

Within seconds, two imposing forms filled the doorway.

CHAPTER 10

Sophie's stomach stopped churning as Quinn and Colton strode inside and sat on the farthest bench from the dais. They wore dusty jeans, denim shirts, scuffed boots, and cowboy hats, obviously having been working on the ranch.

"Are you a ranch hand or the sheriff today, Lodge?" Billy asked from his podium.

Quinn tipped back his gray Stetson and slowly pulled off his leather gloves, his dark gaze meeting Billy's across the room. "I'm always the sheriff to you."

Billy flushed a deep red and glared. "I find it interesting you'd attend today."

"Why?" Colton settled back against the hard wood. "We're concerned citizens."

"Isn't the tribe opposing the development?" Reverend Mosby asked.

Quinn shrugged. "Our attorney can describe our official position when he arrives."

"Your attorney is coming?" Judy said from her seat in the front row.

"Yes. He was a bit farther away and asked us to come and save him a seat," Colton said, his eyes warm on Sophie.

Sophie's heartbeat slowed to just a gallop. She was safe. At least for now. "Are there any more questions about the design?"

A young woman wearing a pink but faded calico dress raised her hand. "Have you conducted any studies about what the development will do to the local tax base? Will our property taxes increase?"

Billy answered before Sophie could. "Of course they'll go up, Jeanine. A high-end country club development with mansions right next door? We'll all pay more just so out-of-towners have a place to golf for a couple of months in the summer."

"What about the lake?" A twenty-something man with long blond hair, faded jeans, and a green flannel shirt hissed out. "Does anybody care that a golf course will do nothing but pollute Mineral Lake with fertilizers, sewer problems, and such? And what about water supply? Our wells go dry now. Add watering a golf course in, and we're screwed."

Sophie placed her hands on the table. "The plan calls for a type-one irrigation system, which basically recycles water, cleans it, and then reuses it to irrigate the golf course. Your wells won't be affected." A rumbling of disbelief filled the room as several people shook their heads. It didn't matter what she said. The crowd didn't want to hear it. Her heart sank. "Are there any more questions?"

Gregton raised his hand again, his eyes lasers through the dim light. "Yeah. How much did you pay to bribe the county commissioners this time?"

A shadow fell across the aisle as Jake asked from the doorway, "What was that?" Danger coated his voice with a softness that slammed silence into the room.

Gregton shifted in his seat, and Sophie fought the urge to cheer.

"Don't tell me you represent the commissioners and are going to sue me for slander," Gregton sneered.

"Yes, I do. And I will sue, if need be." Jake took three steps into the room—all male animal in a deep navy suit with tan silk tie.

Gregton dipped his head toward Sophie. "You gonna sue me on her behalf, too?"

Jake's eyes darkened to coal as he ran his gaze over her from head to toe. He turned back to Gregton and slowly shook his head, his jaw tightening to iron. "No. You insult her, and we're stepping outside."

"Is that a fact?" A thick man next to Gregton clomped to his feet while two others followed suit.

"It is," Jake affirmed.

Quinn and Colton stood and moved behind him. The three brothers formed a powerful wall that gave Sophie the first peace of mind she'd felt all day.

JAKE EYED the crazy son-of-a-bitch and shoved all anger into a box to be dealt with later. It took the combination of his military training and his legal education to keep him from going for Gregton's throat. Even with a strong hold on his temper, chances were blood was going to fly.

The fanatical group used intimidation to get their way, and he doubted bloodshed would bother them much. When he'd heard Sophie had headed to meet with them alone, he'd panicked for the first time in years.

Truly panicked.

Thank goodness for his brothers. Quinn would back him in an instant, even if it meant losing his sheriff's position. Colton would fight to the end for him, too. As Sophie stood so defiantly up front, he wondered who'd fought for her in the past. Suddenly, his chest hurt.

So he smiled to reassure her that he was there for her. "This is over. Come on, Sophie."

She faltered, her blue eyes too big in her pale face. Then she pushed away from the table.

"Now there, boys," Billy said from the podium, his eyes on the crowd. "I believe we're finished with our questions for Miss Smith." He nodded her way. "We appreciate you coming today." His gaze beseeched her to make a quick exit.

"I appreciate your invitation," she murmured while walking into the aisle.

Jake moved slightly to the right so she'd keep her focus on him and not on the angry people.

Relief filtered across her face, and she made it to his side without mishap. When he took her arm and ushered her toward the door, his muscles finally unwound. Several pairs of eyes bored holes into their backs as they left.

She released a pent-up breath as they walked into the sun. "I can't thank you enough."

"So, we're not hitting anyone?" Colton grimaced and stomped toward the chestnut stallion tied to a nearby tree.

"Guess not," Quinn rumbled as he stalked toward his own mount and lifted himself into the saddle. He smiled. "It's always interesting, Sophie."

Jake cleared his throat and tightened his grip around Sophie's upper arm. "Thanks."

Both of his brothers nodded.

Sophie halfheartedly waved as Quinn and Colton rode into the nearby trees. "Thanks for the support."

For now, they needed to get out of there. "Get in your car, and I'll follow you to Shiller's." Jake gave her a gentle push toward her Jeep.

Sophie escaped into the green vehicle and drove toward the

main road and Jake followed, keeping a close eye until they reached Shiller's.

He was out of his truck before she'd even closed the door of her rental car. "What in the hell were you doing meeting with that crazy group all by yourself?" He knew he towered over her, and maybe frightened her, but something in him didn't give a shit. How dare she put herself in such danger?

She shifted so her back rested against the hard metal of the vehicle and shrugged. "They wanted to meet. I didn't know they were nuts."

"They're nuts," Jake confirmed. He had no right to be so angry with her—she wasn't his. Yet tension still squeezed up his throat. "*The Rockefellers* changed their name three years ago. They used to be *the Johnsons.*"

"No." Sophie laughed.

Jake nodded, forcing his shoulders to relax. He had no right to yell at her.

Sophie grabbed his suit lapels with both hands. "I wasn't in any real danger, was I?"

Lust clawed through Jake's gut. If this was her way of appeasing him, it was definitely working. "Probably not. But they're a bit off."

"Yeah, I got that." She lifted smiling eyes to his. "I guess I owe you a thank-you, huh?"

Oh yeah. A thank you sounded nice. "I guess you do."

She tugged. He complied by dipping his head. Sophie stretched to her tiptoes and pressed her lips gently against his. "Thank you." Her voice was husky as she dropped back to her feet.

"You're welcome," Jake murmured. If she thought that was the end of it, then she'd misjudged him. He lowered his head and kissed her, going deep. The woman tasted like strawberries and vanilla, and he wanted to feast for days. Maybe weeks. His hands encircled her waist to pull her against him. Finally, he let her go. "You make up your mind?"

Sophie smoothed out the wrinkles she'd caused. She kept her eyes chest level. "Still mulling it over."

Jake stepped back and released her waist before placing one knuckle under her chin and lifting her face until her gaze met his. "Take your time, Soph." He'd learned patience as a lawyer and knew when to back off—which is why he always won. Sophie's acquiescence was much more important than any case he'd ever taken, and finesse was necessary. "I need to get to court. I'll call you later."

He jumped into his truck, not looking back. If he looked back, no way would he leave. The woman had to make up her own mind to come to him. When she did—then he'd take over.

SATURDAY NIGHT ARRIVED, and again, Sophie had once again agreed to dinner with Jake. It was as if she *wanted* to get her heart smashed.

She'd spent Friday alternating between designing the garden, playing in her sketchbook, and pondering Jake's proposal. The time would soon come for her to make a decision. She wanted him, without question, but the last thing she needed was a broken heart. Yet a fantastic night with a hard-bodied cowboy, one with obvious intelligence, might be too difficult to pass up.

For years, she could remember that night fondly. Right?

She wore a light pink skirt with deep blue blouse for dinner, and she waited for him on the porch swing. Her new boots finished the outfit perfectly.

Tall, broad, yet somehow graceful, he approached from his truck, a sexy predator in civilized clothing.

She smiled from her perch on the swing. "I have something for you."

"What's that?" His boots made dull *thuds* as he crossed the painted wood.

She handed him the charcoal drawing of Leila with her pretty hair in ribboned braids, her eyes sparking with spirit and intelligence as she won a new foal from her uncle. Softly rounded cheeks and delicate features hinted at the lovely woman who would one day emerge from the impish body.

The scents of natural pine and wild berries lifted the air around them as Jake accepted her gift.

"Sophie," Jake breathed, holding the thick paper at arm's length. "It's beautiful. *She's* beautiful. Thank you." His eyes warmed her.

He really liked her work. Delight flashed through her as she accepted his hand and walked to the truck. They drove for a while, both lost in their own thoughts, and Sophie stilled in surprise when he pulled into his long driveway.

"I'm cooking you dinner." Intimacy and something deeper wove through his words. Sophie took a deep breath. "I won't push you. Just dinner." He enfolded her hand with his larger one.

She nodded. The need to see where he lived, where he slept, propelled her from the truck. Thick logs made a three-story home with large wraparound porch and deep green door. A massive three-car garage sat apart from the house to the right.

"That's a big house," she murmured.

Jake nodded. "I grew up here. Mom moved to Tom's when they married. I bought out my siblings when I married Emily."

"Where do your siblings live?" Sophie climbed the burnished oak steps.

"Colton plans to build a house over behind the east ridge with a great view of the lake, and Quinn already built his over on the south side next to the river. It's closer to town so he can get there in a hurry if they need the sheriff. Dawn still lives at home and hopefully will until she's forty." He opened the heavy door and gestured her inside. "We own the ranch equally, so whoever's working it takes a salary, and then we split the profits or losses."

"Wow. That's great that you guys split it so fairly." Renewed longing for a family washed through her.

"How else would we have done it?" he asked.

Sophie turned and gasped at the amazing view. While Loni's house overlooked the valley and Mineral Lake on the north side, Jake's home overlooked it from the northwest. The mountains extended well into Canada in the distance.

"It's beautiful," she breathed. "I'd love to paint this scene."

"You should." Jake closed the door behind them. "I've seen your work. You should paint all the time."

There he went again, making her feel strong and talented. A girl could get used to such security.

She smiled at the comfortable room laid out similarly to Loni's. Big stone fireplaces must be required during the cold Montana winters. Thick green couches, Western oil paintings, and floor-to-ceiling windows made the house a home. She followed Jake into a pale yellow and tan kitchen and through an open sliding glass door onto a huge cherry-wood deck. The glass table was set for two with the candles flickering in the twilight hour, and the smell of barbecued steaks filled the air.

"Sit." Jake pulled a chair out for her, and she sat, her gaze still on the amazing view. The lake and mountains looked too still to be real. Too beautiful with the vibrant pink and orange sunset to exist naturally.

Jake brought side dishes out from the kitchen and then flipped open the barbecue lid and speared a steak for her plate. He filled his own and took a seat across from her, pouring the wine.

"This looks great, Jake," she murmured.

"So do you." His gaze roamed her face over his wineglass. Heat and interest combined into an irresistible invitation in his fathomless eyes.

Desire skipped past humming to raging within her in no time. How did he do that?

They ate in silence, comfortable in the warm night. The food was delicious.

Jake refilled their wineglasses. "Are you ready for the hearing Monday night?"

"I think so. My part is just describing the golf course and maybe the clubhouse." She took a sip of the red wine. "Are you going to be there?"

"Yes."

Her hand stilled. "Opposing me?"

"No. Opposing the location of the Charleton Group's development," he said.

She set down her wineglass. "That's me."

"No, it isn't. I want to make you happy, Sophie. But a golf course does not belong so close to Mineral Lake." His tone was firm.

Her heart hitched. "I don't like being on opposing sides from you."

Jake grinned. "Worked for Hepburn and Tracy."

She reclaimed her wineglass. The thought of sparring with him thrummed awareness through her veins. "Where's Leila?"

He leaned back in his chair. "Girls' night at Mom's." He continued at her inquisitive look. "Don't ask me. Mom, Leila, and Dawn all paint nails, do hair, eat popcorn, and who knows what else. Girl stuff."

"Sounds like fun." Wistfulness filled her tone, unbidden.

"I'm sure you could join them sometime. Though if you talk about boys, I'd trick a rundown from my daughter. Maybe my mother, too."

Sophie rolled her eyes.

"Why don't you paint more? You're an amazing artist." He smoothly switched topics.

Pleasure flushed her at the compliment but then quickly died. "Artists don't make any money, Jake. I need security and my job provides that."

Coal-dark eyes surveyed her. "Those words don't sound like you. They're not yours, are they?"

"Of course they are." Sophie tossed her napkin on her plate and pushed back from the table. "I'll clear these for you."

One strong hand around her wrist stopped her. Then he tugged, and she lost her balance. Straight onto his lap.

"I'm sorry if I upset you." His mouth was an inch from her ear. Heat and hard masculinity surrounded her, and she repressed a groan. She perched on granite-hard thighs against a too-warm chest as firm arms held her tightly. As if he'd never let go.

She turned her face to meet his. "I'm not upset." Breathiness quieted her voice.

"Whose words were they, Sophie?" His eyes held hers captive while he shifted her into a more comfortable position.

The need to confide in him swelled. "My mother's."

"Do you still believe them?" he asked.

Right now, she was finding it difficult to believe anything. To concentrate on anything but the talented lips of the man before her. She had known what would happen when she accepted his dinner invitation. She leaned forward and pressed her mouth against his, her hands splaying against firm pectoral muscles earned on the ranch.

Jake stiffened, one hand moving to cup her head and ease her back enough for their gazes to meet. "Are you sure?"

"Yes." It came out a breathless dare.

He didn't ask again.

CHAPTER 11

*S*he met him halfway as his mouth plundered, as his tongue explored. He smoothly shifted her so she faced him, her thighs on either side of his, her core to his. One hand went to her hips and pulled her even tighter into his hardness.

They both groaned at the contact.

Strong hands deftly released the buttons of her blouse. He pressed hard kisses along her jawline and down her neck. Each touch of his lips sizzled against her skin. A wildness filled her—a sense of power she hadn't expected. He flicked her bra open with a quick movement, and her breasts spilled into the cooling night.

"So pretty," Jake murmured.

His heated mouth enclosed one nipple in heat. She gasped and gyrated against him. She was already wetter than she'd ever been.

He ran his tongue around her nipple, his teeth scraping.

Her breath caught. Reaching out, she shot both hands through his thick hair. "Let's go inside."

Releasing her, he leaned back. "No."

She opened her mouth, but no sound emerged. So much hunger filled her it was hard to concentrate.

He gripped her waist. Then he easily lifted her until her butt hit the table. His strength sent butterflies winging through her. Then his nimble fingers skimmed across her nipples. "We need to get you out of your head, Sunshine."

She shook her head, her mind spinning, her body on fire. "No, we don't." She gasped more than said the words. The chilled glass cooling her thighs contrasted with his heated hands on her breasts.

His smile gleamed with predatory charm. "Spread your legs."

Her eyes widened. Half naked, exposed on his table, her mind rebelled. They were outside, and while his deck seemed secluded, his family or ranch hands could walk into the backyard at any time. "No."

He rolled her nipples. Pain and pleasure melded together, shooting electricity straight to her pounding clit. She gasped, her lids lowering to half-mast. Her hands lifted.

"Hands down." His order held bite and her hands slapped the glass.

Then he tugged her breasts just enough to show he was serious. "I said, spread your legs."

Like prey in a trap, she stilled. He'd let her leave if she wanted—heck, he'd drive her home. The next moment was hers to control. If she stayed, she'd give up control to the force of nature that was Jake Lodge. His sensual gaze promised dark pleasure, but at what cost?

Need trembled through her. The man could quench the fire he'd already stoked in her. Her body leaped to life with desire for his sexy promise, while her brain bellowed caution.

Screw her brain.

She panted, lifting her breasts even as he kept his hold. Licking her lips, she hesitantly, sensually, widened her knees.

He blinked. Slowly.

Her skirt rose up her thighs. Her ankles dangled on either side of his chair. Lowering her chin, she met his gaze with as much challenge as she could throw from her eyes. He wanted control? The man had better earn it.

He shot to his feet. Fast. The man was *fast*. Keeping her gaze, he leaned over her and shoved plates off the table. They crashed to the wooden deck, shattering. Surprised, she dropped back on her elbows and gasped.

Heat cascaded off him and onto her bare skin. Sliding his palms along her arms, he removed her shirt and bra.

She trembled.

He leaned closer, trapping her. Crimson spiraled across his high cheekbones, enhancing the dangerous hollows in his chiseled face. His calloused hands manacled her thighs.

She jerked. Desire uncoiled inside her abdomen with the force of nature. Thunder rolled in the distance, in tandem with the slamming of her heart.

Pinning her with a look, he ran his abrasive palms up the flesh of her thighs. His hips kept her open, his gaze kept her captive.

She bit back a whimper.

Pure instinct tilted her pelvis toward him.

"Hold still, Sophie," he commanded softly.

Her breath hitched. Hold still? No way. She shook her head.

"Yes." He ran a thumb along the outside of her panties.

Nerves fired to life. Her body trembled with the urge to move. "Please—"

"No." He leaned over her and kissed from her collarbone to her jugular. "The begging comes later," he whispered in her ear.

His heated breath shivered along every nerve she owned. "W-who do you think will be begging?" she forced out.

He moved her panties and plunged one strong finger inside her.

She cried out, sparks flashing behind her eyes. Her orgasm

was so close. Needing to move against him, she nearly hissed in frustration.

His finger rotated. "I believe you'll be begging." Low, guttural, his voice rasped with hunger.

A strangled moan slipped from her mouth.

"Now that's a pretty sound." He released her to tug off her panties and skirt, leaving her completely nude. Lust glimmered in his eyes as he looked his fill in the waning light. "You're stunning."

For the first time in her life, she felt stunning. Beautiful and somehow...safe.

His hand curled around her nape, gripping just hard enough to show his strength. Then he caressed his rough palm down between her breasts, over her tightening abdominal muscles, to stop at her mound, his heated gaze following his touch.

She started to shake with a need that bordered on painful.

The lingering daylight faded, leaving his face shrouded in darkness. The moon lit him from behind, a strong, dangerous figure who held her captive in his spell. He was as wild as the land that had created him.

So much for safety.

He dropped back to his chair, his hand planting under her butt.

Panic seized her. She struggled to sit up, even with her legs dangling over the table. "No—"

His thumb pressed on her clit just as his mouth found her.

She arched her back with a garbled cry. Mini-explosions rippled through her—not enough. Not even close to enough.

He licked her again. "Lay back down."

It was too much. "No—"

His hard hand slapped her clit.

The world sheeted white and went silent. She dropped on her back, lost in the erotic sensations he'd created.

His mouth found her again. A low hum against her vibrated through her entire body. She teetered on an edge, a fine, dangerous brink. More than anything in the world, she wanted to go over.

But that pinnacle lay within Jake's control. At the thought, her need spiraled even higher.

His finger entered her. Easily. Another finger—stretching her. Pain and pleasure spasmed through her. Then his rough tongue flicked and caressed her clit. Circling. Tempting and teasing. Her muscles tightened, her abdomen rolled.

He sucked.

The universe detonated. She arched her back, screaming his name. Explosions of electrical fire roared through her, sparking every nerve, shaking every muscle. Hot pleasure rippled through her and crested into waves.

He worked her, prolonging the orgasm until she really did want to beg.

Finally, the waves settled. Her body relaxed on the table, her muscles turned to mush.

Wetness coated her face. Her eyes fluttered open. Was she crying? No. Then she frowned. "When did it start raining?"

He chuckled, finally releasing her to stand. "The rain started a minute ago." Drawing her toward him, he lifted her against him. Her thighs settled against his hips, and she clasped her ankles behind his back as he kissed her again.

Aftershocks of pleasure rippled through her sex. More. She needed more.

He lifted his head, his grin pure sin. "Hold on."

She nodded before lowering her mouth to his neck. He tasted of salt and man—earthy and sensual. The corded muscle along his neck and jaw tempted her to nibble and nip, uncaring of their movements.

Of where he was taking her.

The scrape of a door failed to stop her exploration until the world shifted and she found herself on her back, spread out on a comfortable bedspread.

Rain glistened in Jake's darkened hair, while hunger flared in his eyes. He stood by the bed and ripped his shirt over his head.

Such raw strength hitched her breath.

She couldn't match him. A tornado couldn't match him. "Um—"

"I'll keep you safe."

He slowly drew his belt free of his pant loops, the leather whipping through with a whisper that caressed down her body. After unsnapping his jeans, he kicked free of his clothing.

She swallowed. His cock was solid and huge. He reached into a side table for protection and rolled on a condom. Settling on his knees on the bed, he lowered himself so they were flesh to flesh.

She moaned in pleasure at his heavy weight, her nipples scraping against his hard chest.

Finally, she could explore him. Hard ridges of muscle filled her palms when she ran them across his chest. He vibrated, barely civilized, barely contained.

Then, his muscles bunching, his forehead sweating, he slowly, purposefully entered her, inch by swollen inch.

"Jake, hurry up," Sophie groaned, digging her fingers into his shoulders.

"Patience." He dropped his forehead to hers. "I don't want to hurt you."

"You won't." Her words emerged garbled and breathy.

He chuckled against her lips and then kissed her deep and sure. With a hard push, he embedded himself fully in her. Man, he was big. Almost too much. "Are you all right?"

Concern from the strong, controlled man above her shot emotion straight to her heart. Right where she didn't want it to go. "If you don't move, I really am going to hurt you," she hissed.

His dimple dared her to try it. She nipped his bottom lip. His eyes darkened to liquid midnight. One hand held her hip in place. The other tangled in her hair. "You were being so good. Now you don't get to move." His hand moved around and clasped her butt.

"Not a chance." She tried to move against him.

He kept her in place.

Fire rushed down her torso.

His weight pinned her, the hand in her curls tethered her, and the hand at her butt kept her still. He was in complete control. He waited, his gaze determined, his focus absolutely on her.

At least a minute passed.

Finally, she relaxed beneath him. Obeyed his silent demand to submit. She could trust him—and she did.

He moved her against him. Then moved faster. Then started to pound. As he took over her body, he breached her last emotional shield. Heat coiled inside her, rolling outward, powerful waves lighting her nerves. She exploded. Tears filled her eyes as the intense ripples devastated her.

He thrust harder, prolonging her orgasm, filling the world with Jake Lodge. Finally, with a low growl of her name against her skin, he leaped into pleasure with her.

Exhaustion shuttered her eyes closed before he'd removed the condom and tucked her close. He smoothed a kiss against her damp forehead. "Go to sleep, sweetheart."

This was too much, but she was too tired to deal with any emotion. In the morning, she'd figure everything out, and right now, she was just going to enjoy the hard-bodied cowboy. Allowing herself to feel protected, she turned boneless. Warm and safe, she stretched into oblivion.

Sophie awoke to a large hand idly caressing her hair on the pillow. Her back was pressed against his broad chest, and contentment flowed around her, through her. She slowly stretched sore muscles that hadn't been used in much too long. And never like that. Jake had awoken her three other times during the wonderfully long night, and it was well worth it each time.

"Good morning." His voice rumbled with sleep.

"Morning." She snuggled into his warmth and stilled as parts of him hardened instantly. "What are you, a machine?"

He chuckled. "No. All of me just likes all of you. A lot."

"Ditto." She stretched like a lazy cat with a big yawn.

"We have to talk," he said.

Uh oh. Not exactly what a girl wanted to hear after an incredible night of sweaty sex. "'Bout what?" She masked her yawn this time.

"The condom broke."

"Which condom?" Her brain was too fuzzy to capture his meaning.

Strong arms tightened around her. "The third one."

"Oh." Reality slammed with a *thud* as her eyes focused on the painting of a desert landscape on the opposite wall. Thick rust and orange cascaded in firm swipes illustrating hard rock. "The condom broke."

"Yes," he said.

"Inside me."

"Yes."

Intellectually, she understood that condoms were only ninety-eight percent effective, even if used perfectly. So two out of a hundred uses failed. But still, she trusted them. "Oh," she murmured.

His hand resumed playing in her curls. "How's the timing on that? You know, cycle wise?"

Her heart pretty much stopped beating. "Ah, the timing." She calculated in her head. Once and then again. "Um, the timing would be ideal if we were planning to procreate."

He stiffened behind her. Not in the good way. "Ideal, huh?"

"Yes." Dread made her limbs heavy. "But, hey. No worries to you. Really. I've got this." Could this be any more awkward? One smooth motion had her under him. All of him. Amusement warred with intent in his eyes. "You've got this?"

"Uh, yeah." She nodded vigorously against the pillow, her face aching as embarrassment spiraled heat into her cheeks. She bravely met his gaze even as her breasts pebbled in response to his welcome weight. Condoms broke—it was possible, even in this day and age. The warning was on the box, for goodness sakes.

"Sophie?" He lowered his face. His muscled body pressed her into the mattress. "Do you think you've gotten to know me during the time we've spent together?"

She groaned. Even with the recent revelation of a broken condom, her body reacted to the feeling of him against her. She fought to keep from moving against him. From stretching up into his heat. "Yes?"

Jake's jaw firmed. "If you had to guess, how do you think I'd react to your statement?"

"My statement saying that I got this?" Her voice whooshed out in a breathy whisper. She tried to concentrate on the subject at hand. Instead of the hardness caressing her flesh.

"That statement," he said.

"Um. Not so good?" she whispered.

His eyes glittered in the morning light. "Not so good," Jake affirmed.

"Ah. Sorry."

"If you are pregnant," Jake said, enunciating each word, "we will deal with it together." He pressed a hard kiss against her lips. "Got it?"

She gave up the fight and moved against his hard erection. "Yes."

His gaze was intent. "Sophie?"

"Yes?" She moved again.

"Are you trying to distract me?" he asked.

"No. I'm trying to motivate you. Is it working?"

His eyes flared, hot and bright. "Yes."

"Thank God. Use *an unbreakable* condom this time," she said.

CHAPTER 12

*M*onday morning, when she ran out to the Jeep to search for her missing sunglasses, she found a third note on her windshield. This one was even more threatening. *Last chance. You don't want to ruin the land. I don't want to ruin you.*

Should she tell Jake? Or the sheriff?

She stuffed the note in her purse and spent the day preparing for the hearing that night. She'd call Quinn tomorrow.

The doorbell chimed as evening approached, and she flew down the stairs to keep from disturbing Mrs. Shiller, who'd caught a cold. Her exhibits were already lined up at the door, and she needed to get going. Now. She opened the door and stopped cold.

"Preston." Seeing Aquaman on her doorstep wouldn't have shocked her as much.

"I flew in with the Charleton Group's attorneys, grabbed a car, and came to surprise you. Surprise." Sunlight glinted off his silver watch as he leaned forward to peck her on the cheek. His beautiful suit with a Burberry tie complemented his deep eyes and wavy blond hair, and he looked as out of place on Mrs. Shiller's country porch as a scarecrow by the Eiffel Tower.

Relief filled her that she wouldn't be alone. "I'm surprised."

"I thought you could use moral support tonight. Are you ready?" He lifted foam boards she'd stacked by the door.

"Yes." She grabbed her purse off the floor and followed him to a silver Jaguar.

Sophie handed over the remaining exhibits, sank into the front seat, and squirmed. Her uncle's company must really need the job if Preston had left a city for the country. "You rented a Jag in Maverick, Montana?" she asked.

"There was only one, pretty lady." Preston shut her door, placed the colorful boards into the trunk of his car, and climbed into the driver's seat. "We can celebrate later tonight."

Her mind reeled. She had enough to worry about without hurting Preston's feelings about the cruise. No way could she go with him now, considering she'd had crazy monkey sex with Jake Lodge last night. "I'm sure I can catch a ride home. I think my friend Loni will be there."

Thunder rumbled in the distance as Preston maneuvered the sleek vehicle through the windy road past town. "How have you managed this last week? I thought I was kidding when I asked how you were enjoying visiting the middle of nowhere." A hard rain began pelting the car, and he flipped on the wipers.

"It's peaceful here." How could he not see the quaint tranquility of the town? A jagged arc of lightning lit the forest on either side of the narrow road and belied her words.

"So is the moon, but I don't want to live there," Preston said tersely. "The casino is on the other side of the reservation?"

Sophie shivered in her white summer suit as the night grew even darker outside the purring vehicle. "The casino is another twenty miles on the way to North Dakota."

"I did some checking and the tribe wants to build its own golf course on the other side of the land, away from the lake.

They're supposed to break ground in the next few months," Preston said.

The saliva dried up in her mouth. "Are you sure?"

"Yes," he said.

If Jake was fighting her for monetary reasons and not *for the land*, she'd kick his butt.

"Why don't you fly home with me tomorrow? The commissioners might not make a decision for another week." Preston wrenched the wheel to the left as a branch crashed onto the road, scattering green pine needles every direction.

"Actually, I thought I'd stay. I was hired to design a memorial garden and should be able to finish it this week." She'd come up with a great plan and couldn't wait to share it.

Preston glanced down at her. "Hired? By whom?"

"My friend Loni."

Preston stiffened. "Is she from Maverick?"

"No. She's on the tribal council," Sophie admitted.

"Sophia. They're on the opposite side of us on this," Preston drawled.

Just because the tribe opposed one of her clients didn't mean the tribe couldn't also be her client. Plus, she wanted to create that garden. "They're not involved in the golf course design. The tribe is a separate entity, just like any other citizen, and it happens to oppose the proposal. It's not us against the tribe…"

Preston's knuckles whitened on the steering wheel. "Are you sure about that? I heard their lawyer is ruthless."

"Jake Lodge." Just saying his name skittered heat across her lower belly.

"Yes. Jake Lodge."

Town lights came into view, and Sophie shook her head. "Jake isn't like that." He couldn't be. He was a good guy.

"You sound like you know him, Sophia." Preston's voice lowered to a timbre she'd never heard before.

She shifted uncomfortably in her plush seat. "For the love of Pete. Would you please stop calling me Sophia?"

"That's your name."

She hunched her shoulders, feeling like an idiot for not complaining sooner. "I prefer to be called Sophie."

"Why didn't you ever say anything?" he asked.

"I don't know. Sophia sounded right coming from you." Until Jake Lodge came into her life.

"What is going on with you, Soph…ie?" Preston parked in front of the brick County Justice Building. Fat raindrops plopped onto the windshield, and the wind rattled against the glass.

Sophie could only shrug as she jumped out of the car and looked up at the five-story stately brick building presiding over Main Street. Preston retrieved the exhibits from the trunk, and they dashed inside the double doors.

She smoothed her white pencil skirt as her tan pumps clacked on the wood floor while she followed signs to the public meeting room. Her stomach dropped at the sheer number of utilitarian blue chairs lined up in rows.

Preston lifted a hand for two men seated at a long table and nudged Sophie in their direction. She skirted the rows of chairs and strode toward them.

"Miss Smith." Oliver Winston stood and smiled. Sophie shook his hand, having met the Charleton Group's managing partner several times while creating her design. Stateliness defined him in his burnished brown suit with D&G loafers, and his Rolex shot prisms of light around the room. His red tie appeared to be hand-sewn silk. "This is Niles Jansten, our attorney," he added.

Niles took her hand in a firm grip—almost too firm. Shrewd brown eyes set in an aristocratic face matched a silk tie screaming money. His eyes roamed from her eyes to her breasts, and Sophie removed her hand.

She gave a silent prayer of thanks she was seated between Preston and Oliver.

Niles said, "First I'll introduce the development, and then Miss Smith will show her design to the commissioners. They may or may not ask questions at that time. Then the public will testify. Most will babble on about how development, any development, is bad. The commissioners have heard it all before." He gave Sophie a quick once-over and she fought an irritated shiver. "Then I'll have a few minutes to rebut all of that and we're off."

"What about the tribe?" Oliver murmured.

Niles tapped his watch. "Either they'll all testify with the public, or just one representative will testify on behalf of the entire tribe. It could go either way."

"I think their attorney will be testifying." Preston turned to watch the public file in and take seats.

"Oh good. A country lawyer to deal with. Can't wait," Niles sneered under his breath.

Preston raised an eyebrow. "Not so sure Jake Lodge is an ordinary country lawyer, Niles."

"We'll see. Please tell me he'll be wearing cowboy boots," Niles muttered.

"Actually, I've seen him in slate gray Armani." Sophie kept a smile plastered on her face. "Though I doubt we'll see that tonight."

"Why not?" Niles asked.

She crossed her sandaled feet under the table. "The crowd is small town. The commissioners will be as well, I assume."

Preston nodded next to her. "Good point. We're overdressed, aren't we?"

"I'm not." She nodded toward a group of newcomers. "There's Jake Lodge." Chocolate Dockers over buffed brown cowboy boots showed long and lean legs. His crisp white dress shirt with red tie emphasized his tanned face and strong jawline, while his navy sports coat accentuated his muscled torso. His jet-black hair was tied back at the nape, giving him a primitive appearance. His brothers, Hawk, the chief, and his parents filed in behind him, along with several other members of the tribe.

"He certainly has presence." Preston settled back in his chair and laid a casual arm along the back of hers.

Coal-black eyes instantly shot their way. Sophie straightened in her seat and her heart dropped to her stomach. Jake said something to his family, his gaze holding hers across the room. The others began to take their seats.

Jake started forward, forging a path directly toward them.

CHAPTER 13

*S*everal people nodded to Jake, but nobody attempted to stop his forward movement. Sophie couldn't blame them. The look in his eyes warned of determination, and she had the oddest urge to ask Preston to remove his arm from her chair.

"So that's how it is," Preston murmured. "I had a feeling…"

Energy emanated around Jake when he reached her table. "Did you drive here in that storm, Sunshine?"

"No, I drove her." Preston stood and extended a hand. "Preston Jacoby."

"Jake Lodge." The men shook hands. There was no question they were sizing each other up. "I played the Mintwell Island course you designed outside of D.C. It was a great challenge," Jake said.

"Thanks. You like a challenge, Lodge?" Preston smiled.

Jake showed his teeth. "Haven't lost one yet."

"There's always a first time." The men released each other.

Jake nodded. "Not now. Stakes are too high, sport."

Sophie's stomach dropped. They weren't talking about the golf course anymore. If they ever had been.

Jake turned to the other men. "You must be Oliver Winston and Niles Jacoby."

Surprise flashed across Niles's face. "You do your research, Mr. Lodge."

"Of course." Jake dismissed the men with a quick grin at Sophie. "Good luck with your presentation." He moved away after saying to Preston, "I'll make sure she gets home tonight." He returned to his family and took his seat.

Loni waved at Sophie and mouthed, *Good luck*. Colton gave her a wide smile, Quinn nodded, and the chief winked. Several other people she had met at the branding picnic found their seats. Ignoring the knotting in her stomach as people filled the room to capacity, Sophie waved back at several of them.

Three county commissioners entered through a side door. First came Madge Milston, a pretty white-haired ex-librarian, then Jem McNast, a silver-haired farmer from outside Maverick, and finally Jonny Phillips, the retired high school football coach. Sophie had done her research on each of them.

Madge introduced the board and set forth the rules for the hearing. Then she called Niles to the podium.

"He's good, isn't he?" Preston whispered about halfway through the presentation. Sophie nodded. Niles's lengthy PowerPoint presentation illustrated the Group's other developments as well as the economic advantages it had brought to other areas. He showed beautiful homes, golf courses, and views. Finally, he turned the podium over to Sophie.

Her knees wobbled. Taking a deep breath, she stood and maneuvered around chairs to the front of the room. Squaring her shoulders, she placed exhibits that showed the layout of the golf course, the clubhouse, and some possible home sites on the easels behind the podium. She gave a quick speech, recapping what Niles had said.

She answered the board's questions regarding setback

requirements, golf course maintenance, and preservation of indigenous trees.

"Did you draw those, young lady?" Commissioner Phillips asked, pushing his spectacles up on his nose while pointing to the detailed drawings of the eighteenth hole and clubhouse.

"Yes, I did, Commissioner," she said.

"They're just beautiful, dear." Commissioner Milston smiled. "I heard you're designing the garden for Willa."

Sophie's spine prickled with awareness. "Yes, Commissioner," she said slowly.

"You know, we should have a nice garden on the other side of Maverick, don't you think?" Madge Milston asked the other two members of the board, both of whom nodded instantly.

Sophie scrambled for a way to stay on topic. "Well, both the golf course development and a community garden would draw tourists to the area, not only for day trips but for longer periods of time."

"That is so true," Commissioner Phillips agreed. "We'll have to get together and see what kind of funds we can obtain." He coughed. "Do you plan on having those pretty fish ponds at Willa's Garden?"

"Um, yes." She disliked losing control of the meeting, although being treated like one of the community tickled her. She cleared her throat. "Commissioners, if there are no more questions about this design, I'll turn the podium over to the public."

The board nodded, and Sophie escaped back to her seat. She didn't need to look to know Jake's amused eyes tracked her progress.

Several members of the public asked for a halt to all development. Some complained the golf course was too far from town, while others argued it was too close and would cause traffic problems. The Concerned Citizens Group sat toward the back, and only Billy Rockefeller testified about the perils of government control and why Montana needed a citizens' militia. The board looked as if it had heard it all before.

Finally, Jake's name was called.

He strolled like a lazy panther to the podium, all grace and confidence. An unwelcome hum whispered through Sophie's blood. The hum pooled in a very private area as memories from her time in his bed flashed through her mind.

"Commissioners, I'm Jake Lodge, and I represent the Kooskia Tribe tonight." He placed a stack of papers on the podium, but his earnest gaze stayed on the commissioners. "The tribe opposes the development. First, as you know, we own Mineral Lake just below the proposed site." Several tribal members nodded their heads in the audience. "Now, the last thing we would ever want would be to sue the county for allowing a development to pollute the lake."

Sophie tensed. Jake's threats chilled her desire.

"Damn," Preston breathed next to her. "He did not just threaten to sue the entire county if the development is approved."

The commissioners straightened to focus on his testimony. "Jake, are you really saying you'd sue the county?" Commissioner Milston looked down her librarian nose at him, and Sophie fought a smile. Retirement hadn't diminished that look at all.

"You know we take preservation of Mineral Lake very seriously, Commissioner. You bet we'd sue the county, as well as the developer and every applicable land owner, should the lake be threatened."

"Young man, I don't appreciate being threatened," Commissioner Phillips noted.

Jake smiled. "I understand, Commissioner, but I had an excellent football coach who once taught me that hiding your game plan wasted time. It was better to lay it out there, show your strengths, and you'd know right off where you stood in battle. It's a lesson I took straight to the Supreme Court."

Commissioner Phillips's eyes warmed, and his lips twitched.

Jake turned toward Commissioner Milston. "A savvy librarian once chastised me for tricking a girl into the back stacks. She told me that if I wanted to kiss a girl, I should just say so and not create a story. That way the girl could make up her mind and I'd know the attraction was mutual."

He turned then, his gaze warming on Sophie for a heartbeat. She swallowed, unable to move.

Then he focused back on the county commissioners. "I'm just saying what's what so the county isn't surprised by future repercussions."

He turned to Commissioner McNast while Milston smiled at him in exasperation. "Also, I spent more than one very hot, very tiring summer moving watering pipes to irrigate fields of hay and wheat while learning to respect the land around us." Jake embodied intelligence and intriguing charm as he spoke. "Those pipes didn't have wheels like they do today. It was unhook, lift, move, and hook again."

A couple of knowing laughs came from the audience.

"But," Jake said, turning serious, "I learned that if you pay attention, the land will show you what's right. Geography will show you where to place the pipe, where the water needs to spray. In this case, we need to look at the land and preserve it for future generations. I know Mineral Lake is as important to Maverick County as it is to the tribe." Several heads nodded. "Besides the lake, the tribe has serious concerns with this particular developer."

Sophie's stomach dropped. Thank goodness she was sitting.

"What do you mean, Jake?" Commissioner Milston pulled papers closer to her face.

"I mean that the Charleton Group is known for pitching one

design and then building another once a permit has been granted." He punched in a couple of keys on the computer next to him and a golf course design came up on the big screen in the corner. "This design shows a golf course with homes set every acre apart and was approved in Michigan three years ago." He hit a couple of buttons. "This is the actual development." It was still a golf course, but four-story condominiums lined the sides. Jake showed three more examples, all with the same result. "All of these were developed by the Charleton Group." A muted gasp arose from the crowd.

Then Jake turned to Sophie. "Miss Smith's golf course is beautiful and is designed for homes to be scattered every two acres, right?"

Sophie nodded, fighting the urge to push back from the table. To put distance between herself and the man commanding the podium. Sharp hurt angled through her chest.

"Now, Miss Smith, would your design work if condominiums replaced the homes?" he asked.

All eyes turned to Sophie, but she only saw the black ones pinning her. He was hard and cold. Determined. A slow anger started to build between her shoulder blades and pushed the hurt aside. For now.

"Miss Smith?" he asked again.

How dare he put her on the spot like this? Every muscle tightened in her body, her eyes shooting sparks at his. They'd shared a bed. The things she'd let him do to her! "My design includes homes every two acres."

"I understand that." His voice gentled. "That wasn't my question. I asked you whether or not your design would work with condominiums."

Sophie was silent for a moment as she struggled for the right answer. His look told her he'd wait all night. Her chin lifted. They were so freaking done. "No. My design would not work with condos."

"Why not?" he asked.

The bastard. He was going to get her fired. But the truth was the truth, and she wouldn't lie to the county. "The setbacks would be off. The golf course is designed to complement the lake, which would be blocked by condominiums." Strength infused her voice as she met his challenge. No way would she let him see the pain he'd just caused. She'd trusted him.

"Did you know?" His voice lowered even more. They could've been the only two people in the entire room.

"Know what?" She didn't like this Jake. The same mouth that had explored her the other night was set in a firm, uncompromising line. He looked big. And dangerous. Exuding a threatening undertone of anger if she answered wrong.

His eyes went flat. "Did you know that the Charleton Group usually alters designs after county approval?" he asked.

"Of course not." How could he think that? Hurt made her sway in her chair. She'd looked over many of their finished projects, and that had never happened. But they'd commissioned tons of designs, and she surely hadn't studied them all.

Niles jumped to his feet. "We've had enough of this slander. I can assure you, Mr. Lodge, you can expect a lawsuit from this."

Jake's eyes didn't leave Sophie's face as he replied, "Truth is an absolute defense to slander. In other words, bring it on." Then he gathered his papers, nodded at the commissioners, and retook his seat.

Niles turned toward the commissioners. "The tribe opposes our development because it wants to build a golf course over by the casino."

Commissioner Milston turned toward Jake. "Is that true, Jake?"

Jake stood. His voice easily reached around the room, even without the microphone at the podium. "I stated why the tribe opposes the project, Commissioner. It's bad for the land, and a shady developer is bad for the county."

Preston hissed out breath as Jake continued. "However, as

you are well aware, the tribe has made no secret of its plans for the casino, hotel, and golf course. We do plan to put in a golf course." He flicked a glance their way. "I'm sure you are also aware that two, even three, golf courses in close proximity actually benefit them all. We'd like to be a golf course haven. People could stay at the hotel for several days and play several different courses."

"Bullshit," Niles muttered under his breath as he sat.

Sophie clasped her hands together under the table to keep them from shaking. To keep anyone else from seeing them shake.

"Still think he's a nice guy?" Preston whispered dryly.

"Is he right about the condominiums?" she asked under her breath.

"Not to my knowledge, but we'll definitely have to follow up on this," Preston said.

Madge banged a gavel and said they would issue a decision within a week. They stood, and the crowd began to mill around Jake, everyone talking at once.

"You have to get me out of here," Sophie whispered to Preston.

"Of course," he said.

Loni suddenly appeared across the table. "Oh, there you are, Sophie. I drove myself in today. Would you mind driving home with me? I came in earlier to do some shopping and didn't know the storm was coming. I'll drive, but I really can't see very well at night and the boys all brought their own cars. I just don't want to go alone." Guileless brown eyes beseeched her.

When Preston started to speak, Sophie held up a hand. "Of course I'll drive with you, Loni. Let me grab my exhibits and we'll go." Loni was safe. Sophie needed time to think. Time away from Preston—and Jake.

"I'll help." Loni hurried over to the easels.

Sophie turned to Preston. "It's okay. I'll call you tomorrow."

"Are you sure?" he asked.

"Yes." She had to get out of there before Jake escaped from his admirers.

"If you're certain. Don't worry, Sophie. It'll all work out." Preston dropped a light kiss on her forehead.

The fury leaping into Jake's dark eyes across the room snared Sophie's gaze. She instinctively moved away from Preston and toward the exhibits. "Let's go," she whispered to the older woman. With a concerned look at her son, Loni let Sophie tug her out a side exit while Jake remained stuck in the crowd.

Sophie breathed a sigh of relief when they were finally alone on the road home.

As Loni maneuvered the car onto the freeway, Sophie watched the flicker of lights across her friend's face.

"I'm not sure what I should say," Loni said softly, her eyes intent on the wet asphalt.

"There isn't anything to say," Sophie returned.

Loni's hands tightened on the wheel. "He was just doing his job," she said.

"It was more than that," Sophie muttered.

"It *was* more than that." Loni's brow wrinkled. "Jake, his heritage, it's important to him. Mineral Lake and the land, plus the future of the tribe. He's a fighter, my Jake is."

Sophie's nerves jerked until she wanted to puke. "The tribe is everything to him."

"Not everything. Family is right up there. Of course, the two usually combine."

Sophie stared miserably out the window as drops of rain began to fall again. His heritage was everything to him, and he'd really turned into a shark at that meeting.

She didn't know the real Jake Lodge at all. One day he was a gentle cowboy who cooked her dinner and made love to her. The next he became the cold, methodical lawyer, taking the Charleton Group apart piece by piece. Or was he the powerful cowboy controlling a wild stallion with his thighs? Whoever he was, the man would win. Would do anything to win.

She just couldn't be pregnant. She couldn't have a man like that in her life controlling her. Controlling her baby. What was she even worrying about? It was one broken condom. The idea that she'd be pregnant was crazy, and she needed to just relax and forget about it. She needed to forget about Jake, too.

She didn't notice as Loni stopped at the B&B.

"Will you be okay tonight?" Loni asked.

"I'll be fine. Thanks for the ride," Sophie said woodenly as she grabbed her exhibits from the backseat and ducked into the rain. She kept her head down against the deluge as she crossed the walk and climbed the steps to the front door. After she turned to wave, Loni flashed her lights and headed down the road.

Sophie put her boards on the porch, shifted to unlock the door, and jumped when a voice interrupted her thoughts.

"Running, are we, Sunshine?" Jake asked from the darkness.

CHAPTER 14

*S*ophie pivoted, safe from the rain beneath the porch overhang. The shadows sat comfortably across the hard planes of Jake's face, his back against the porch swing, his long legs extended to cross at booted ankles. He was relaxed, a predator surveying its prey. "I think we should talk, don't you?

"No, I really don't think so." She turned back toward the door and stiffened as the swing moved. Hurt and fury commingled until she wasn't sure what she'd do. "How did you beat us here?"

"Back roads. My mom drives slowly... I don't."

She'd kick him in the groin. Yeah. Good plan. "Whatever. Go away," she said.

"It was business." He stood right behind her, his breath warming the top of her wet head.

She didn't turn around. "Baloney."

"Maybe not completely," he admitted.

Her breath fogged the square pane of window. A part of her wanted his reassurance that their night together mattered. "You didn't have to put me on the spot."

"No, but I knew you'd tell the truth and that most of the crowd already liked and trusted you," he said.

An unwelcome warmth spiraled through her. She was such a dope. "Sounds like a calculating, strategic move, Jake."

"Maybe." His hand latched on her elbow and swung her around. "But it was the truth."

Fury heated her face and cascaded down her spine. "Was it? How about the tribe's golf course? Afraid of a little competition?"

"Not in the slightest." His calm demeanor was going to get him punched. "I meant what I said. An additional golf course would only draw more tourists to the area. Look at Coeur d'Alene, Idaho. There are at least nine golf courses within fifteen miles of one another; some you can see across the lake from others. I told you our reasons for opposing your project."

"Why didn't you tell me the tribe planned a golf course?" she asked.

His chin lowered. "I am a lawyer, darlin'."

"Yeah, well, I must have forgotten that." Sophie jumped as thunder rumbled directly overhead and gusts of wind sprayed rain at them. It matched the fury screaming through her blood. She gestured toward the rainy night while jerking her hand from his grip and stomping a safe distance away. "Even the weather worked to your advantage—I saw your mother home."

"Thank you. I believe she was trying to help you." Rain dripped from the rapidly curling hair across his forehead. The scent of man and musk filled the space. "You think I control the weather now?"

Sophie squeezed the water out of her wet curls. "I'm sure you'd like to control even the weather, but that seems to be out of your reach."

"*You're* not," he said in a low timbre.

"Not what?" she asked.

A swift arm grasped her and yanked her into his hard body. "Out of my reach."

Sophie put both hands on his chest and pushed. Hard.

His only reaction was a slow, dangerous smile that set her heart sputtering. "Brute strength isn't how you'll get what you want."

"Oh, but it is for you?" Her hands clenched with the need to belt him.

A nonchalant shrug and raised eyebrow belied the seriousness of his gaze. "If need be."

"Meaning what?" His hands burned through her linen jacket and matched the heat flowing through her blood. Her body thrummed to life, her nipples peaking in contrast to the anger rippling through her. What was wrong with her?

"Meaning…" His hands tightened imperceptibly on her upper arms as his face dipped to within an inch of hers. "If Preston puts his mouth on you again, he'll be gumming his food for the immediate future."

"Y-you wouldn't."

His gaze hardened ever more as one hand lifted to tangle in her wet curls. "Wouldn't I?"

Erotic tingles cascaded along her scalp. The man was beyond male. Primitive and powerful.

A satisfied glint lit his dark eyes as he gave one short nod. "I don't share. You would do well to remember that."

She couldn't help it. He'd done nothing but push her all night, and she was just done thinking. Done trying to do the right thing. Just done. Going on instinct, she grabbed his shirt and leaned up, kissing him as hard as she could.

He paused for one second. Then his mouth took over. He wasn't gentle. And he wasn't sweet.

The kiss was all fire, depth, and strength. Desire speared directly south through her as one broad hand went to the front of her blouse and snapped the buttons free. She groaned as his mouth abandoned hers to trail hard, sharp kisses along her jawline and down her neck before both hands ripped her shirt apart. He roughly cupped her bra-covered breasts.

Then he paused. "Are you sure?"

"Yes." She pushed into his hands, groaning at the contact. "I'm sure. Though I plan to kick you really hard later."

"It's a date, then." One quick flick of a finger and the front clasp opened, spilling her flesh into waiting hands. Into warm hands that instantly, expertly, molded her to him.

This was crazy. The road may be quiet this time of night, but anybody could drive by. Oh, she could stop him, but nothing in her wanted to do so.

His head dipped. Liquid heat engulfed her nipple, and she cried out. How was his mouth so hot? His tongue flicked her even as his hands manacled her hips to hold her in place. Jake was all fire.

Suddenly, she was lifted into the air. Her shoulders smacked against the wall. She wrapped her legs around his hips as the rough wooden planks of the old house scratched her back.

She should be yelling at him. But need—a dangerous, dark, primal need—had her in its grasp. Or maybe she'd jumped headfirst into desire. Either way, she was tired of thinking. Tired of being alone. Tired of taking the safe route.

She yanked his shirt over his head. Dark smoothness filled her aching palms. She ran them urgently over the tight muscles of his chest. He was hard. And strong. Everywhere she was soft. Even with her head spinning, she marveled at the differences between them. Wanted more. Wanted everything.

He'd hurt her at the hearing. A feminine part of her needed reassurance…needed to know she mattered. But even deeper, a hunger uncoiled inside her that only Jake Lodge could appease.

So he damn well would.

She stiffened when he snapped her thong in two. His hand found her, and she bit her lip. He cupped her, his index finger sliding easily into her heat. Mini-explosions rippled through her sex.

A soft gasp escaped her lips to echo in the night. She leaned her head against the ridges of the house, her eyes fluttering shut. Her hairclip dropped to the floor, and her hair tumbled free. "Don't stop," she breathed.

"Didn't plan on it," he said, rough and amused.

She almost swore as his hand left her aching, needing more. Then she helped him make short work of his pants and boxers before he shifted and impaled her against the wall.

"Oh God," Sophie whimpered.

He more than filled her. The vein in his shaft pulsed deep inside her. One hand seized her ass, holding her in place. The other hand threaded through her hair and twisted.

Her neck elongated, while she clawed his rock-hard shoulders.

His broad chest lifted as he inhaled slowly. Nearly nose-to-nose, he caged her in place, his body warming hers. A small scar near his ear gave him an even more dangerous edge. Even his ridiculously long eyelashes only served to enhance the hard angles of his face. The firm set of his jaw matched the determined glint in his midnight eyes.

"Now we talk," he said very softly.

A shiver wound down her spine. Her sex gripped his cock, and her thighs undulated with the need to move. Fast and hard. "No. No talking." Not while he was inside her, slowly killing her.

His absolute focus landed on her, gaze piercing hers. "I'm sorry if I upset you at the hearing."

No way. He did not get to slam inside her, until all she wanted was him to move, and then apologize. "Fuck you, Lodge," she gasped out.

Amusement creased his cheek. "In a minute."

She coughed out a laugh. "Don't be cute."

"I can't help it." He pulled out and then slid back in. Sparks of intense pleasure lit her from inside. "I'm sorry I hurt your feelings."

"If you truly hurt me, I'll destroy you." The man had just been doing his job—and he hadn't really come after her, just the Charleton Group. She squeezed her internal walls around his shaft.

His nostrils flared. "I think that's fair, sweetheart." He started to move.

She tightened her hold, lifting her pelvis. Sensation after sensation rammed against her clit. Her eyes closed. Sparks flashed behind her lids.

He increased his speed, easily holding her in place. His strength impressed her. His hands entranced her. But the tension spiraling deep inside stole every thought from her mind. She wanted what he promised. It was the light at the end of a railroad tunnel—the final plunge of a roller coaster—the slash of yellow through deep gray clouds.

It was so close.

Plunging even harder into her heated core, Jake gave her what she sought when his mouth took her nipple. With a sharp nip of his teeth, Sophie's world spun away from her. From reality.

She cried out his name as the orgasm beat through her with merciless intensity, as she saw stars. Jake followed her into oblivion with a groan that sounded like her name. His head dropped to the curve of her neck, dripping cool rain down her back in contrast to the heated lips claiming the area between her neck and shoulder.

Sophie came down from bliss to the smell of rain, pine, and man. She lifted heavy eyelids and masculine satisfaction met her gaze without apology.

She shivered as the cold wall along her back and buttocks permeated her fog. Jake lowered her to the floor, then pulled her skirt back into place. Sophie stood motionless as big, gentle hands fixed her bra and straightened her shirt. The sweet kiss he placed on her swollen lips shot tears to her eyes.

"I'm not letting you go, Sophie," he murmured.

"Yes, you are." There was no half loving Jake Lodge. He was an all-or-nothing type of guy. She couldn't take the risk. She pushed back with both hands.

This time, he moved. "Meaning?"

"This is over," she said, aftermaths of her orgasm still rocketing through her.

A raised eyebrow met her declaration.

"I mean it." Her mind spun as her heart ached. "I am leaving. We just had sex on a porch, without protection. Again."

Jake straightened. "We did."

"At this rate, there's no way I won't get pregnant. We're done. You said it yourself—we'd have some fun until I left."

"You're not leaving yet," he said slowly.

"I don't care. It's wild and exciting but...I don't want to get hurt. I'm not made for this." It was way past time to protect her heart. Though something told her that it was too late. Way too late.

Jake's eyes softened in the dim light. "You might be pregnant."

"Please. Statistically, it's improbable. Even so, we'll deal with that if and when." She felt small and vulnerable in the dark night.

"It'll be all right." Promise whispered through his deep voice as he turned her toward the door, shielding her from the storm. "I promise."

CHAPTER 15

*P*reston's phone call woke Sophie from a dead sleep the next morning. She blinked at the early morning light as it hazed through gauzy curtains. She reached for the cell, her mumbled "Hello" nearly a hiss.

"Hi, Sophie." The sounds of traffic and people filled the background. Preston raised his voice. "We're at the airport on the way back to San Francisco, and I just wanted to call and let you know."

"What's the plan?" She sat up and placed her back against the brass bedrail. Curls tumbled forward and she swatted them out of her eyes.

"We have a late afternoon meeting with the rest of the Charleton Group. Niles wants to discredit Jake Lodge before the commissioners make up their minds."

Unease folded Sophie's hand into a fist. "Do you think he'll be able to do it?"

"No," Preston said flatly. "I researched the guy. Lodge is solid." He paused for a couple of beats. "He seems like one of the good guys."

Right. If only she could totally believe that statement. "I'm not so sure about that."

"If you need anything, and I mean anything, promise you'll call. Until you give me a definitive answer, I'm keeping the booking on the cruise. Things will look better once you're home where you belong," Preston said.

"I will, thanks." She disengaged the call and got out of bed. The sooner she finished with Willa's Garden, the sooner she could get home. She grabbed her toiletries and headed for the shower.

An hour later, Sophie crept quietly down the hall, not wanting to wake Mrs. Shiller.

"Hello there, dear." Mrs. Shiller poked her bespectacled face out of the kitchen at the bottom of the stairs. "I have huckleberry pancakes and fresh coffee coming up."

Sophie inhaled the sweet aroma of the purplish fruit filling the air as she descended the steps. She walked into the kitchen and took a seat at the large wooden table. Five places with delicate Prince Edward floral china perched atop linen placemats.

"Are we getting more guests?" she asked while pouring herself a cup of coffee from the old blue cast-iron pot.

"I have some friends coming for breakfast since I'm feeling better today." Mrs. Shiller bustled around the kitchen. "I hope that's okay? I'm known for my hotcakes." A pretty pink blush filled her papery face as she placed butter and syrup on the table.

"The more the merrier," Sophie said. Nothing like coffee and pancakes to brighten a girl's day.

Voices filled the entryway in the other room. "Oh good, here they are." Mrs. Shiller smiled as Commissioner Milston and a tall, slender woman entered the room. "Sophie, you know Commissioner Milston, and this is our friend Juliet Montgomery."

"Call me Madge," the commissioner said with a soft smile as she took a seat at the table.

This was unexpected. "Okay, Madge," Sophie agreed slowly. "I'm not sure we can really talk until you render a decision."

Madge helped herself to some coffee. "Oh, of course we can talk. Just not about your golf course proposal." On her slim form, a black silk tank top sat comfortably over black silk shorts and red sandals. She looked more like the sexy type of retired librarian than the stodgy one.

"Well, that makes sense." As much as anything else did these days.

"It's nice to meet you," Juliet murmured as she took a seat. She looked to be in her twenties with red hair and deep blue eyes. She wore a long flowered skirt, blue peasant blouse, and dangly silver earrings. A silver Celtic knotted pendant hung from a thick silver chain around her neck.

Mrs. Shiller set an overflowing platter of pancakes in the middle of the table. "Dig in, ladies. Loni is running late this morning."

"Loni is coming?" Sophie accepted the platter from Juliet. She dropped three cakes onto her plate before passing it to Madge. "Why do I have the feeling this is more than friends gathering for breakfast?" Had she and Jake been seen last night? Having wild sex against the house?

Mrs. Shiller twittered as she sat next to Madge. "This is just breakfast. There's really no reason to turn bright red, Sophie. My goodness. Are you all right?"

"Fine," Sophie choked out while grabbing her coffee cup for a deep swallow. She was saved from scrutiny by the front door banging shut. Though it wasn't Loni who strolled in.

"Why, Sheriff, what a pleasant surprise." Madge smiled.

Mrs. Shiller moved to rise from the table. "Yes, would you like to join us for pancakes?"

"No thank you, Mrs. Shiller." Quinn gestured for the older

woman to sit. "I have a meeting with Fish and Wildlife in five minutes but wanted to give Miss Montgomery these papers." He extended a stack of official-looking papers to the young woman sitting as if frozen at the table.

Crimson covered Juliet's pretty face as she accepted the stack. "Thank you, Sheriff."

Sophie felt for the woman but was relieved to be out of the limelight. Today Quinn looked like a tough country sheriff should. Long and lean with faded jeans, gray cowboy boots, and a thick blue button-down shirt open at the collar that emphasized his deep black eyes. A mean-looking gun rode his hip, appearing for all the world like it belonged just there.

"Are those the reports on the break-in?" Mrs. Shiller leaned forward.

"Yes." Juliet glanced at the papers. "Have you arrested anybody?"

Quinn shook his head. "Not yet, but we have two suspects in custody. A couple of kids from Billings looking for quick money to buy drugs. We're waiting for one to crack." He ran a hand through his hair. "Read those over, sign your statement if it's correct, and we'll meet up later today to talk about it." He turned toward the door.

"I'll just give them to Loni after our meeting today," Juliet said, her eyes still on the paper.

Quinn stopped at the kitchen doorway and turned, one dark eyebrow raised, his square jaw set hard. In that moment, Sophie could see the resemblance between the brothers. "No. Be at my office at noon, Juliet." Then, he was gone.

Sophie broke the uncomfortable silence hanging in Quinn's wake. "He reminds me of his brother."

"Pain in the butt," Juliet said with an eye roll.

Sophie shared a grin with the redhead. "Exactly." Odd as it seemed, in that moment, she made a friend.

"Well, I wouldn't mind having that kind of a problem." Mrs. Shilling tittered, her eyes on her pancakes.

"Amen, sister," Madge agreed as she dug in. "Though I'm sorry about the break-in at the gallery, Juliet. Were many paintings taken?"

Sophie swallowed a bit of huckleberry flavored heaven. "What gallery?"

"I own the Maverick Art Gallery." Juliet wiped her mouth on a frilly napkin. "I lost one painting and one statue in the robbery. Hopefully they'll be recovered."

How terrifying. "You were at the gallery during the break-in?" Sophie asked, her eyes wide.

"Well, not really. I have a small apartment above it, so I was at home. Didn't hear a thing, either." Juliet returned to her breakfast, her shoulders hunched.

The discussion concluded as the front door closed quietly, and Loni rushed into the room. "You started without me." She took the final seat at the table and reached for the platter of pancakes.

"The hotcakes were ready." Mrs. Shiller passed butter and syrup toward her friend.

"Have you asked Sophie?" Loni asked before taking a bite and closing her eyes in bliss.

Sophie narrowed her gaze. "Asked Sophie what?"

Loni's eyes popped open in surprise. "Oh. Hmm. Guess not."

"We were waiting for you." Madge nudged Loni with an elbow. "Plus, we watched Quinn try to boss Juliet around first."

"Those boys, I don't know where they get it." Loni shook her braided head.

Twin humphs of disbelief came from Mrs. Shiller and Madge.

Loni rolled her eyes. "Here's the deal, Sophie. Juliet owns an art gallery and has promised us a showing of art depicting

Maverick County, the Kooskia Tribe, and the Montana wilderness."

"That's a great idea." Sophie hoped she'd get a chance to see the artwork before leaving town.

Loni turned back to her breakfast. "It's all settled, then."

"Ah, wait there, Loni." Juliet sat forward. "I haven't seen Sophie's work yet."

Sophie took a drink of coffee. "My work? Why would you see my work?"

"Of course." Loni nodded. "Sophie, would you go grab your sketchbooks for Juliet? Then we should probably come up with some sort of timetable."

"Wait a minute. My work? Timetable? What exactly is going on here?" Sophie set her cup down with a dull *thud*.

Juliet tilted her head to the side. "You said she was on board for the project, Madge."

Madge shrugged and concentrated on the bite remaining on her plate.

"Why, you're our artist. I thought that was obvious." Loni gestured to Mrs. Shiller, who rose from the table and exited the room.

Sophie shook her head in disbelief. "I'm not an artist. I'm a landscape architect specializing in golf course design."

"You're an artist working as a landscape architect. Your heart and soul belong to your craft. Anybody can see that," Loni said.

"Loni—" Sophie began.

Mrs. Shiller returned with Sophie's large sketchbook and handed it to Juliet. "Sophie left her pad in the parlor last night. Here we are."

"Is it okay?" Juliet asked quietly.

Sophie blinked several times, overwhelmed by the compelling force of the women around her. "S-sure, I guess." Her stomach dropped as Juliet flipped open the cover. Juliet was a real gallery owner. What if she thought Sophie sucked?

Loni breathed out at the charcoal drawing of Colton standing tall, amusement dancing in his eyes. "That's him. That captures him so perfectly." She made similar comments as Juliet flipped the pages one by one.

"It's me!" Mrs. Shiller exclaimed at the sketch with soft sunlight sparkling over her face as she kneaded bread.

"Look at Tom." Loni's eyes softened at the portrait of her husband perched on a paddocked white fence. "And me." She turned smiling eyes on Sophie.

She had captured Loni watching her sons at the picnic with a mixture of love and resignation.

"Oh my," Madge murmured at the charcoal of Jake staring out of the page. Determination lit his eyes while strength ruled his face—all male, all warrior. "Look at that man."

Juliet closed the book. "These are incredible. Do you also work in oils?"

Hope flared to life in Sophie's chest. She didn't even try to quash it. "Yes. Watercolors, too."

"You have the showing if you want it." Juliet gave her a slightly apologetic wince.

"She wants it," Loni chimed in as both Madge and Mrs. Shiller clapped.

Sophie rose from the table. "Now wait a minute. A project like that would take a year, maybe two. I'm only here for another week, ladies." She carried her empty plate to the sink to rinse off and felt the silent communication going on behind her.

"Will you at least think about it?" Loni asked.

"I'll think about it." Sophie wouldn't be able to think about anything else. She kinked her neck to the side before turning around. A real art showing—of her work. The thought was beyond anything she'd dared to dream about.

If she wasn't careful, however, Maverick Montana would become too wonderful to leave. She had to return home. Right?

JAKE FOUND Sophie sketching in an alcove in Shiller's backyard. She sat on a stone platform surrounded by rose bushes, climbing flowers, and greenery, looking like a sexy and magical sprite. "I decline your offer," he said softly, tucking his hands in his jeans.

She started and glanced up, her eyes refocusing. "What offer?"

"When you said we're over last night. I decline." He'd spent a restless night trying to figure out how to change her mind, and finally decided the direct approach would be best.

Her grin flashed a flirty dimple. "It wasn't an offer—it was a statement."

That dimple roared a hunger through him that weakened his knees and hardened his cock. "Then I reject your statement."

She closed the sketchbook, her gaze dropping to the bulge in his jeans. "Doesn't look like rejection to me."

Was she being coy? "Don't underestimate me, Soph." It was only fair to give her warning, even while claws of need ripped through him.

She blinked back at him, her eyes darkening to cobalt. "Look who's talking." Desire washed her delicate cheekbones with pink, matching the cute skirt that only went to her knees. Those cowboy boots made her legs look impossibly long.

He could find happiness with this woman. The thought flew out of nowhere, and he batted it away. For now, he just wanted a taste. So he knelt between her legs, his palms skimming up her thighs.

Her eyes widened, and she grabbed his hands. "We're outside."

Ah. He liked her off-balance, so he didn't tell her that Mrs. Shiller was currently playing bridge at Adam's bar. "I know."

"Jake." Her lips parted, lush now with the arousal he could see running through her.

"I do like how you say my name." He shook off her hands and continued his journey, his shoulders forcing her knees farther apart.

Her eyes flicked around the peaceful backyard, even as her nipples hardened beneath his gaze. "I, ah, don't know."

"I do." Her scent was driving him crazy. "All you have to do is say yes." If she pushed him away, he'd need to go jump in the lake to cool off.

She gingerly touched his chin, her gaze blazing. "Every moment with you is something. Yes."

Ah, she was a sweetheart. He leaned in and captured one nipple in his mouth, sucking through her shirt. No bra. His head might just explode. Her fingers tangled in his hair, and she gasped.

His other hand found her, hot and wet. He groaned around her nipple, and her thighs trembled against his arms. She was about as perfect as a woman could be. He abruptly released her, then lifted her shirt over her head.

"Well, okay. I guess we can see each other just until I leave town," she said breathlessly. She fell back onto her elbows, her smile a siren's song. Apparently, for this stolen moment in time, she was willing to forget her vow to leave him.

Keeping her gaze, allowing her to see the hunger raging through him, he slowly unbuckled his belt. He wanted to bury himself in her so deep she'd never consider leaving him. He kicked the jeans and briefs to the rosebushes and slid on a condom. Hopefully this one wouldn't break.

Feminine awareness, feminine strength, glowed hot and bright in her dangerous eyes. Teasing him, she slowly reached under her skirt and tugged her black panties off her legs. Then she smiled.

It was the smile that did it.

Moving so quickly she yelped, he grabbed her up, turned to sit, and slowly, so slowly, lowered her onto his raging dick. She breathed out and yanked his shirt over his head. He rumbled with pleasure when her palms met his pecs.

No way would he go for easy and gentle right now. Later. Much later. Right now, he was burning for her. Her tight body wrapped around him, so much heat, so much grip. Grasping her hips, he lifted her, and then plunged her back down.

Pleasure sparked along his entire shaft. He dropped his head to her neck, nipping.

Nothing felt as good as this moment—as this woman taking him, milking him. His balls drew tight against the base of his cock. She gave a hungry moan and arched.

He yanked her up and back down, snarling at the dark pleasure he felt being so deep inside her. For two heartbeats, he forced himself to stop, to remain still. To just feel.

Her sex clenched him, vibrating around his shaft, rippling over him. "I'd give anything to stay inside you forever—just you and me, feeling you come over and over again," he murmured against her skin.

A long, winding shiver moved up her spine. She whispered his name against his neck as she lifted up and shoved back down.

His hands tightened on her hips, and he set a furious rhythm. Harder, faster, blinding strokes slammed her against him, his thrusts deep and sure. A roaring filled his ears. Heat clawed down his spine to flare in his balls.

She stiffened, crying his name, her internal walls gripping him like a vise. He exploded, lightening flashing through him. Deep, violent spurts tore from him as he held her close.

Finally he relaxed, his knees going weak. His face dropped to the haven where her neck met her shoulder. She panted and huddled against him, her heart beating so rapidly he could feel it in his chest.

There was no way he could let her go.

CHAPTER 16

The week sped by as Sophie finished the design for Willa's Garden to the council's satisfaction. Jake won a local trial and was asked to consult on a trial in D.C. He'd called on his way to the airport to let her know.

Pleasure had filled her that he'd checked in with her before leaving. Just like they were a couple. During that week, it had seemed as if they were. Quick lunches, a few dinners around his hectic schedule, with a hot, hungry cowboy taking her to new heights in his bed afterward. Man, she was lost.

Without Jake around, Sophie used the time to think instead of sleep. She was sketching the porch from the swing one morning when her phone rang.

"How's my favorite girl?" Her uncle's gruff voice charmed through the line.

"Uncle Nathan! How are you?" she asked.

"I'm fine. Just got word—your commissioners denied the development and golf course," he said.

Defeat slumped her shoulders. "I'm so sorry." Would they go bankrupt now? Tears filled her eyes. She wanted to be furious with Jake, but if what he said was true, she couldn't blame him for exposing the group. Though he certainly hadn't needed to use her to do it.

"Not your problem, sweetheart. Had an interesting phone call from a Jake Lodge, however," Nathan said.

"Really?" Suspicion laced her tone.

"Offered to buy your design for a fifty-acre parcel next to some casino," Nathan affirmed

Sophie kicked the wooden floor so the swing started to move. "You're joking."

"Nope. Of course it'll have to be reconfigured for a different space. He also said that you staying on was a condition of the sale, however." Curiosity filled her uncle's tone now.

"Son of a bitch." Her temper ignited until her throat closed. Sure, she had feelings for the lawyer, but nobody manipulated her.

Her uncle chuckled. "I thought you'd be pleased."

"What? Pleased that he's trying to run my life? Trying to keep me here? It isn't bad enough that his mother has given me an art showing, now he's going to buy my services? I don't think so." She kicked the floor harder. It was only because she might be pregnant. He had been more than happy with a short fling before the stupid condom broke.

"What art showing?"

Sophie told her uncle in great detail about the showing, pausing once and again to kick the floor. The swing complained with a soft squeal.

"Wow, Soph. Isn't that what you've always wanted?" he asked.

"What are you talking about? I want to design golf courses." Her protest sounded weak, even to her own ears.

"You like rendering the designs for golf courses. Your favorite part begins when you pull out the colored pencils," he said.

She bit her lip. "So?"

"So, why not give the art a shot?"

Dread filled her. "Are you firing me?"

"Of course not, but I want you to be happy. I'll adore you no matter what you do for a living," Nathan said.

Adoration for her uncle filled her chest. He'd always been there for her. He knew how much she wanted to paint—to be a real artist. But she wouldn't be bullied into it by Jake Lodge, who only wanted to keep his possible kid close. "It's my decision what I do for a living, and nobody is going to railroad me into a career. Any career." The term *so there* echoed in the silence.

"Like your mother?" Nathan asked.

She jolted. "Uncle Nathan—"

"Say the word and you'll have a plane ticket waiting for you at the airline counter. I'll bring you home immediately if you want."

Sophie stopped swinging. If staying in town would save her uncle's company, she'd suck it up and do it. "Are we going bankrupt?"

He coughed. "No. Well, I don't think so. That's not something for you to worry about, sweetheart. I'll take care of it."

"I love you," she whispered.

"I love you, too. Want me to send you a ticket home?"

His unconditional love always gave her a much needed security. "Thanks, but I have some business to take care of here first." Then she would make her own decisions—without any interference.

"Call me if you need me." He ended the call.

Sophie pushed back from the porch swing just as a blue Toyota Sequoia rumbled to a stop behind her Jeep.

Leila waved from the backseat's open window. "We came to take you to lunch. And to see your surprise."

"Hop in." Loni reached across the front seat and pushed open the passenger door.

Sophie wavered at the top of the porch stairs.

"Come on. You get a *surprise*," Leila called out impatiently.

Sophie bounded down the wide steps and hopped into the large SUV.

"We should've called," Loni said as she drove away. "Sorry about the commissioners."

"It wasn't much of a surprise after the hearing, anyway," Sophie admitted.

"Now you can design the tribe's course, right?" Loni asked.

Sophie stiffened. "I don't think so."

"I guess that'll be between you and Jake. " Loni focused intently on her driving. "Should we do lunch first or go see the surprise?"

"The surprise!" Leila chirped from the backseat. "You are going to love it, Sophie."

Sophie turned and smiled at the little girl. "I do love surprises."

"Are you and Daddy getting married?" Wise charcoal eyes twinkled.

Loni gasped out a cough. "Uh, Leila, that's private." She shot a curious sideways glance at Sophie.

"No, it isn't. If Sophie marries Daddy, then I get a mama." Wistfulness filled the girl's tone.

Sophie's heart splintered. "You and I are friends, no matter what."

"Oh. So you won't be my mama." The girl sniffed.

"I'll be your friend," Sophie said softly.

Leila shrugged, crossing her arms. "That'd be good, too. Though Daddy's a catch. Somebody else will marry him and be my mama if you don't."

Loni smothered a laugh with her hand. "How do you know your daddy's a catch?"

Leila clapped her hands together. "Grets's mom said so last week."

"Grets's mom shouldn't say things like that," Loni said.

"Well, Grandma? Is Daddy a catch or not?" Leila asked.

Loni rolled her eyes. "Of course he's a catch."

"Told you, Sophie." Leila giggled.

Sophie turned a surprised glance toward Loni when they entered the drive leading to Jake's house. Loni smiled.

"You could live here. It's pretty great." Leila continued her campaign.

The vehicle rolled to a stop before Jake's expansive home, and Sophie was saved from answering as the little girl released her booster seat and leapt out of the car.

"This way." Loni's eyes sparkled as she exited the car and turned toward the stand-alone garage with triple brown doors.

"My surprise is in the garage?" Sophie asked. Leila placed a small hand in hers, and Sophie's heart swelled.

"No, upstairs." The little girl tugged her toward the stairway to the left of the garage doors then released her to run up and push open the door. Sophie followed at a slower pace with Loni on her heels and gasped as she entered the empty room.

A high-pitched roof and exposed beams gave the shadows angles to play while light filtered in wide windows scattered across all four walls and illuminated the oak floor. Sophie focused on the lone easel set on a drop cloth in the middle of the room.

"Jake always planned to make this into an exercise room, but he uses the gym in town instead. It looks perfect for a studio." Loni's voice echoed around them.

"It is perfect," Sophie breathed, the possibilities entrancing her. "But I don't understand."

Leila's eyes gleamed. "Don't you like it?"

"I love it." Rolling pastures dotted with horses spread out the back window, mountains rose high and proud out the side, and Mineral Lake stretched out to the left. "But Loni—"

Loni opened her arms. "Looks like a nice place to work on

the exhibit for Juliet. The girl really could use a successful launch."

"She could?" Sophie asked.

"She just moved here a few months ago. An exhibit would surely put her in good form. But we hadn't found the right artist. Until now," Loni said.

Sophie's gaze softened on the easel and empty canvas. "I don't know. I'm shocked Jake would create this for me at his house. I mean, we're not really dating or anything." She hadn't decided to do the gallery showing and hadn't agreed to the tribe's golf course—as far as he knew, she was returning to San Francisco soon.

"It's just a great place where you can capture the surrounding area easily, and it wasn't being used. We help each other here, and you needed a place to paint. Although, whether you're dating or not, take that up with Jake. I believe my boy can be extremely persuasive." Loni turned toward the door and beckoned Leila forward. "Where should we take Sophie for lunch?"

SOPHIE WASN'T surprised when her cell phone rang. Jake's deep voice came over the line like warm honey. "How are things?"

"I'm not sure what to say." She leaned against the wall, back in her bedroom at the B&B.

Silence pounded across the line for a minute. "Say about what?"

"The art studio," she said quietly.

"What art studio?" he asked.

She jerked. "Um, the art studio in the top of your garage?"

He cleared his throat. "There's an art studio in my garage?"

"Oh, no." She sank on the bed and yanked a pillow over her face. Jake had no clue. "Your mother and Leila—"

Jake swore. "Aw, shit, Sunshine. I'm sorry. I didn't know."

"I figured that out," she mumbled. For a brief time, she'd thought maybe he was considering something permanent. Heat filled her face until her cheeks ached. What in the world had she been thinking? She hadn't wanted that anyway—the man was too controlling.

"The town, my mother, they love you." Jake sighed. "They interfere, but they mean well."

Could the world just open up and swallow her? Please? "I like them, too," she said.

"Maybe it's a good thing. The studio at my place... In case you're pregnant," he said slowly.

Oh, for goodness sakes. There was no way she was pregnant. "I'm not, and even so, I could be pregnant in San Francisco," she ground out. She threw the pillow across the room.

"A baby needs a father," he said.

"We're way ahead of the issue, here. I am not pregnant. Seriously, Jake. It was one. Well, two, times." Her embarrassment turned to irritation. "Besides, I won't let you manipulate me—trying to buy my design and everything."

There was a shuffling and then, "Damn it. I have to go. But I'm not trying to manipulate you."

"Are, too," she retorted.

"You're impossible. We'll discuss it as soon as I can call back." With that, he disengaged the call.

"Jerk," Sophie muttered into the empty room.

SOPHIE FINISHED the designs for Willa's Garden but neglected to redesign the golf course for the tribe. Jake didn't call, and she told herself she was happy about that. The last thing she wanted was to fight with him. Loni and Leila found an excuse each day to drop by and take her to lunch, and one day the three of them even rode horseback to a picnic spot overlooking Loni and Tom's ranch.

Loni patiently related tribal history, probably to nudge her into doing the paintings, while Leila blatantly brought Jake into every conversation along with not so subtle reminders that if Sophie didn't snatch him up, somebody would.

Sophie found herself wishing the little girl were hers. To love and protect.

Finally, she just couldn't deal with her thoughts alone any longer. The voices in her head were starting to argue with one another. She called the one person in town who might understand. "Juliet? How about we meet for lunch?"

CHAPTER 17

$\mathcal{T}$he Dirt Spoon diner smelled of grease, burgers, and home-cooked food. Sophie settled into the worn booth, careful to avoid the rip in the vinyl. "Thanks for meeting me," she said after they'd ordered.

"I figured you'd want to discuss the art showing." Juliet smiled and unfolded the paper napkin to place on her lap. Her loose dress and Celtic jewelry made her look like an Irish princess.

Sophie almost agreed—almost took the easy out. But it was time to grow a pair, as her uncle always said. "Actually, I, ah, just wanted to talk... I mean, you're new to town, so am I, and I don't really have, I mean, even at home, I don't have—"

"A lot of friends?" Juliet asked, an understanding smile curving her lips.

Sophie sounded like a loser. But she'd never connected with people. Her mother had seen to that. "I don't have many friends at all."

"Me neither." Juliet shrugged. "I'm glad you called me." Her pretty eyes lit up. "That took courage."

More than she knew. "Everyone knows everyone in this

town, and it seems like they all know what's best for everyone else," Sophie said.

"When somebody gives you directions, they always start with, 'Turn left by the field where Sam Boseby's horse died, and then right by the oak tree where Bobby Johnson fell and broke his leg two years ago…'" Juliet said.

Sophie laughed, her shoulders relaxing. "Exactly."

A couple of men in the far booth argued loudly.

Sophie glanced around but couldn't see them. Then they went quiet. Good.

Juliet sipped from a sweating plastic glass. "Jake is out of town?"

"Yes. He's consulting on a trial in D.C." Sophie traced her fingers over the scarred table. "His mom and daughter created a very cool art studio above his garage for me to paint."

"That's wonderful," Juliet said.

"Without telling him," Sophie finished.

Juliet's eyes widened. She covered her mouth, mirth filling her face.

"I know." Heat spiraled into Sophie's cheeks. "I thanked him on the phone."

Juliet snorted and dropped her hand. "You didn't."

"I did." Sophie shook her head. "The poor guy had no clue what I was talking about."

Juliet laughed harder. Finally, she took a deep breath. "This town, I'm telling you. They embrace you and dictate your life. That means they like you. It's nice to belong."

"I know. Even Jake is trying to push me into staying—and it's not like he's made any big declaration of love or anything." As she said the words, the truth of her hurt slammed home.

Juliet sat back as the waitress delivered their club sandwiches and waited until the girl left. "Have *you* declared anything?"

Sophie stilled in bringing her drink to her mouth. "Um, well—"

"That's what I thought." Juliet took a bite and then swallowed. "Those Lodge men."

"Speaking of whom. What's up with you and the sheriff?" Sophie asked.

Juliet flushed a pretty pink. "Nothing. I mean, he's overbearing, bossy, and always around."

"I think you're protesting too much." Sophie chuckled.

"No kidding." Juliet quirked her lip. "He's my landlord, so I have to get along with him."

Sophie took a sip of water. "Your landlord?"

"Yes. The Lodge-Freeze families own more real estate than you'd believe."

That must've been what Dawn meant by family holdings. "Must be nice." Sophie considered her options. "Who knows, maybe I'll sell a painting someday and then, ah, diversify."

"Speaking of which, I saw how your eyes lit up about the art showing."

Sophie blew out a breath. "I'd love to have a real art showing. To paint Montana and have people come and actually want to buy my work. It's a dream I hadn't ever thought I'd get the chance to explore."

Delight danced in Juliet's eyes. "You're saying yes."

"I'm saying yes. I'll do it on my terms, and some of that may mean I take pictures of landscapes here and then paint in San Francisco." At home. Even though it no longer felt like home.

"Fair enough." Juliet glanced back as the men in the far booth grew louder. "What's going on behind us?"

Sophie glanced up as Billy Rockefeller and Fred Gregton exited the far booth. "The guys from the Concerned Citizens for Rural Development Group seem to be having a disagreement." Frowns lined both men's faces. "They're dressed for, ah, war."

The two men wore camo outfits and flak boots. Billy Rockefeller looked a lot more dangerous in the army outfit than he had in the fancy jacket.

He stopped at their table. "Ladies."

Sophie made the introductions, and he shook Juliet's hand. Fred hovered near the counter and didn't approach.

Billy cleared his throat, his eyes piercing. "I heard the county commissioners were smart enough to deny your plan."

Sophie cut her eyes to Juliet. "Good news travels fast."

Billy shifted to reveal a gun in his waistband. "I also heard the tribe is trying to buy your plan. I'd appreciate it if you refused to sell. We don't need a golf course."

"I'll keep that in mind." Sophie's breath caught in her throat as she eyed the gun.

His lip curled and he lowered his flushed face to hers. "I'll do anything to save the environment, lady. Anything."

Sophie saw red at his obvious intimidation tactic. Enough with people pushing her around. Her temper exploded. After grabbing a bottle on the table, she squeezed it in his face. Ketchup squirted out and spread over his forehead.

She gasped.

He hissed and moved to grab her.

Juliet swung her purse, smashing him in the nose. He stumbled back toward the counter, where Fred caught him before he tripped.

Billy started to lunge forward when a sharp voice in the doorway snapped his name.

Everyone froze.

Quinn Lodge stalked up the aisle, his gaze taking in the situation. "What's going on, folks?"

Sophie gulped air and pointed to Billy. "He has a gun in his waistband."

Billy snarled and stepped far enough away from her that Quinn's shoulders relaxed. "I also have a permit, a fact the sheriff is well aware of."

Quinn eyed Juliet and then Sophie. "Are you ladies all right?"

"Fine." Juliet crossed her arms. "This was a little misunderstanding about ketchup. Right?"

Sophie swallowed several times. "Um, right." Actually, she was the one who had committed battery, considering she'd doused the asshole. But he had tried to scare her, so it was probably all right. She glanced at Quinn. "Let's not tell Jake."

Quinn studied her for a moment. "Not a chance, Soph. Not a chance in hell." He took in Juliet's ketchup-covered purse with a raised eyebrow but didn't say a word. Then he waited until the two men left before giving Juliet a hard glance and then sauntering out the door.

After lunch, Sophie drove away from town to make a purchase. It had been enough time, and she just needed confirmation that the broken condom hadn't led to anything. Or the second time against the wall when they'd forgotten protection. There was no way she would buy a pregnancy test in town—the news would be all over within minutes.

The feeling of leaving home grew stronger as she pulled away from Mineral Lake and headed outside of Maverick County, the sharp peaks of mountains providing a shield from rushing winds.

After driving for an hour, she shivered as dark clouds gathered across the sky and figured she'd get back in time for a good storm. Lightning cracked across the sky, and a hard rain began to pound the vehicle. She flipped on the wipers and lights. Her phone rang just as she pulled into Billings, and she accepted the call. "Hello."

"Where are you?" Jake's deep voice stirred something inside her she struggled to suppress.

"Running an errand. Are you back in town?" She was *not* miffed that he hadn't called. Really. Though fury still rode her at his attempted interference in her life. With her job. With her emotions.

"Just got home," he said.

She peered through the rain-soaked windshield for a drugstore. "Great."

"Do you want to meet for dinner?" The low timbre of his voice caused a fluttering in her lower belly that irritated her, pure and simple.

The lights of a store shone through the darkened night. "No. I may be a while."

"I'm sorry I didn't call, Sophie. We worked twenty-hour days to finish the case up in a week." His frustration came clear and sure through the line.

She needed to end this call. "No problem, Jake." She kept her voice casual.

"Sounds like a problem." Silence sprawled across the line. "Where are you?"

If she could take on crazy Billy Rockefeller, she could handle Jake. "None of your business."

"Excuse me?" Heat colored his words, even through the static.

The wind lashed against her windows. "You heard me. Nice offer you made my uncle. You're not running my life."

"Not trying to." His voice dropped an octave.

That tone was a mite too sexy for her to keep angry, darn it. "Good. Well, since we fired the Charleton Group, I'm sure that Uncle Nathan will sell you the design," she said.

"I assumed as much," he admitted.

"Preston will be here working on it, not me," she said.

Several seconds of silence filled the line as Sophie turned into the fully illuminated parking lot.

"No," Jake said calmly.

She switched off the ignition. "What?"

"I said, no. The deal is for you to redesign the course. Not Preston. You designed the original course, the one that fits in well here. We want you to work with your design. Plus, I understand your uncle stands to lose quite a bit of money if that design isn't used," Jake said.

Sophie's temper stirred. "That's blackmail."

"No, it isn't. It just makes sense to have the original designer alter the same course. Now, where are you?"

"Bite me, Jake." She ended the call and powered down the phone. Not the most mature response, but he deserved it. She squared her shoulders for courage and jumped into the rain to dash into the drugstore.

⚜ ⚜ ⚜

THE SMALL BAG sat like a stone in her purse during a quiet dinner at a small diner just outside of Maverick County. When she finished eating and paid the check, she figured she'd stalled enough. She needed to find out now, because there was a fairly good chance Jake would be waiting for her at Mrs. Shiller's.

She marched slowly into the small bathroom and dug into the bag. She opened the box and read the instructions. Not too difficult. Holding her breath, she peed on the stick. Then she placed it on the back of the sink, turned around, and thrummed her fingers against her arm. She waited a minute. Then another minute, her eyes sightless on the pale yellow walls.

Someone tried to open the door and the lock jiggled.

They'd have to come back.

Finally, three minutes were up. Sophie took a deep breath and turned around to read the test. Through the control window on the stick, a plus sign glowed in bright pink.

She was pregnant.

CHAPTER 18

Fifteen stunned minutes later, she found herself in the Jeep headed toward Mineral Lake. "I'll have to schedule a doctor's appointment." She had been talking to herself for several moments but didn't think it mattered much at that point. Statistically, the pregnancy was just unreal, but it happened. She couldn't believe it. Rain slashed the car while thunder rumbled overhead, but neither pierced her calm. "A good doctor. One with experience. Lots of it."

The windshield wipers made a comforting swishing sound against the glass. "I wonder if it's a girl or a boy."

The car crawled through the deluge as she crossed into Maverick County and then finally the town of Mineral Lake, an odd sense of relief filling her.

"You'll be a member of a tribe, baby, and," she mused idly, "I think that means extra scholarships for college. Among other things." She turned onto her street and parked by the B&B. "Look. There's Daddy waiting on the porch. Wow. Daddy's pissed." She felt drunk. Why should she feel intoxicated? She only drank lemonade at dinner.

Jake opened her door before she could. One strong hand

around her arm helped her to the protected porch. "Where in the hell have you been?"

Sophie stared up into his furious face, her eyes blinking as if in a dream. "The city."

"You drove from town in that?" He gestured toward the driving rain.

"Yes."

He put both hands on her arms, obviously fighting the urge to shake her. "Why?"

"I'm pregnant, Jake." Then she pitched forward and darkness overtook her.

JAKE DODGED FORWARD and caught Sophie before she hit the hard wood porch. Pregnant. The woman said she was pregnant. The odds were so against it, he truly hadn't thought she'd be with child. Condoms broke all the time. Jesus. She was really pregnant?

He cradled her easily, fumbled for the doorknob, and moved them both inside. She felt too small—too fragile in his arms.

A baby. Another baby.

He shook his head. Pleasure flushed through him along with unease. As he looked down at her pale face, something in his chest tightened. He wanted this baby. He wanted this woman.

Setting her down on the sofa, he reached for his phone to call the doctor. She shouldn't have fainted like that, should she? His gut clenched hard. Everything had to be okay. Sophie was just surprised by the pregnancy. And tired. He needed to make sure she got more rest.

The nurse answered, and he made his request. Thank goodness for small towns and good friends. The doctor would arrive soon.

Jake dropped to his knees and smoothed Sophie's hair off her forehead. They should get married.

He closed his eyes and took a deep breath. His one marriage had begun the same way and ended in disaster. What mattered was Sophie, this baby, and Leila. He'd do what was best for all of them.

What was best?

"Sophie, wake up," he murmured.

She didn't move, and fear caught him by the throat. He took another deep breath. Sometimes faints took a while to awaken from. She was fine. She had to be fine.

They'd have the doctor examine her, and then they'd come up with a plan. He was born to strategize, and this was no different than a trial. Okay. Considering it was his entire life, it was a little different. But he could make it work.

They'd come up with a plan, and it'd be a good one. Deep down at his core, he knew he'd never let her go. Now all he had to do was convince her.

SOPHIE AWOKE SOMETIME LATER LAID out on Mrs. Shiller's flowered couch with a cold cloth pressed against her eyes. She flopped a hand on the cloth and tugged it across her face to drop on the floor. Her eyes met Jake's as he knelt by the couch.

"Feeling better?" His voice was soft—his eyes hot.

She pushed to a seated position and dropped her head into her hands. Then she struggled to reach her feet. "Yes."

"No, wait a minute." One gentle hand pressed down on her shoulder. "Give it a minute. You were out for some time."

She shrugged off his hand and the pleasure of seeing him again in the flesh. "I'm fine." As much as she hated to admit it, she had missed his solid presence, his reassuring strength.

"We'll see." Lights cascaded through the window, and a car

pulled through the puddles. The splash of the tires echoed even through the storm. Jake ran a rough hand through his thick hair. "Doc Mooncaller just arrived."

Sophie brushed wet curls off her face. "You called the doctor?"

"Of course I called the doctor," Jake growled. "You just passed out."

"I'm fine. Tell him to go away." Panic spiraled through her. She had never quite gotten over the fear of doctors and needles.

Jake stood and strode to open the door, letting rain blow in from outside. "No."

"Hey, Jake." A portly man with a long gray braid moved gracefully into the room, black bag in hand. Kind brown eyes shifted to Sophie. "You must be Sophie."

Sophie eyed the stairs. "Yes." Maybe she could escape to her room.

"This is Doc Mooncaller." Jake closed the door with a muted *click*.

The doctor crossed and bent down to one knee in front of her. "Rumor has it you fainted, young lady."

"She's pregnant." Jake leaned against the door, broad arms across a muscular chest.

Sophie gave him a baleful glare. Weren't lawyers supposed to be good at keeping secrets? "He's guarding the way out," Sophie whispered to the doctor, rolling her eyes.

The doctor chuckled. "Why, you going to run?"

"I might," she muttered.

Twinkling eyes met hers. "Good luck with that. How far along are you?"

"A couple of weeks." She swallowed, her stomach churning.

He pressed a steady hand against her forehead. "Just found out?"

"Yes." She fought to keep her voice normal.

He reached into his bag for a stethoscope, which he pressed to her chest. "Tired?"

"Yes." Yes, but that might be from fighting her attraction to the pissed-off lawyer.

"Overwhelmed?" the doctor asked.

"Yes." Her voice thickened this time.

The doctor reached out gentle hands and pressed lightly along her neck and glands. "Feeling dizzy now?"

"No," she said.

He left the stethoscope hanging from his neck. "It's time for you to get some rest, dear. Things will be better tomorrow." He stood, his knees popping. "I'd like to see you for a full examination tomorrow—say, after breakfast?"

"She'll be there." Jake moved away from the door.

"She needs peace, Jake." The doctor placed a hand on Jake's arm while opening the door. "Don't upset her." With that, the doctor escaped into the stormy night.

Silence ticked across the room before Jake moved toward her, bent, and lifted her.

"I can walk." Why did it have to feel so good to be in his arms? Solid and warm, the man provided a comfort she could become addicted to.

He climbed the stairs to her bedroom and laid her gently on the bed. "I know." We can talk about this tomorrow.

"You're not sleeping here." Alarm flared in her as he shrugged out of his shirt. Jake didn't answer as his hands went to his belt. She sat up. "I mean it. Mrs. Shiller would be shocked."

His jeans hit the floor. "Mrs. Shiller and her friend, Lily Roundbird, left this morning."

"Oh. I forgot about their week-long trip to Yellowstone." Sophie relaxed. Though the man still didn't need to stay.

"They spend more time in the various casinos on the way

down, and probably just a day at Yellowstone." He kicked his pants to the side.

Sophie sat still as stone while Jake gently pulled her shirt off and tugged his much bigger one over her head and threaded her arms through. Once again, her body won over her mind. She wanted to be held. Heck, she needed it. "I'm not living in Montana."

"We'll figure that out, too." He dragged the covers over them. Then he tucked her into his large body and warmth enfolded her.

She couldn't have remained awake if her life depended on it. "Where's Leila?"

"At mom's," Jake said.

Okay, then. She dropped into sleep as smoothly as warm cream from a pitcher, toasty and safe in Jake's arms.

Her sleep was a dreamless one.

Orange blossoms and spice swirled around her as she struggled to awaken. She opened one eyelid to see a thick mug.

"Wake up, sweetheart. We have a doctor's appointment," Jake said, his voice deep and strong.

Sophie groaned and rolled over before yanking the pillow atop her head. It was instantly removed. "I am not getting up." She curled into a ball and leaped for dreamland.

"Yes, you are." After placing the cup on the nightstand, he lifted her from the bed.

"No." She snuggled her face into a warm chest.

He lowered her until her feet rested on the smooth floor. "Yes."

She groaned as her feet cooled, and she pushed away from Jake. "I'm pregnant, and I need sleep." It was a last-ditch effort that resulted in a deep male chuckle.

"Nice try. Drink your tea, and I'll make my famous scrambled eggs while you shower."

She opened blurry eyes on a freshly showered man, and her libido picked up. Just a bit. "Your scrambled eggs are famous?"

"Extremely," Jake said solemnly with a twinkle in his eyes. "If I leave, do you promise not to go back to bed?"

Sophie looked longingly at the bed and then at Jake's determined face. "Fine," she huffed and turned to grab her toiletry bag, "but those eggs better be worth it." She stomped out of the room and headed for a warm shower.

An hour later found her refreshed and dressed. She sat at the table, her stomach growling in response to the aromatic concoction on the stove.

"You're a bit of a grouch in the morning." Jake failed to hide his grin as he dumped scrambled eggs with ham, onions, and cheese onto a plate before her.

"Am not," Sophie said before taking a healthy bite of eggs and closing her eyes in appreciation. "I'm tired. And pregnant." She glared at him before taking another big bite.

He took a drink of what smelled like coffee. "So this morning attitude is new?"

"Not exactly." She didn't want to give up caffeine but orange juice was good, too.

Jake wisely sat and ate his eggs in silence, pausing from time to time to make sure she ate hers.

Sophie leaned back in her chair, her stomach all but bursting. "So you've been to the Supreme Court?"

"Twice." Jake took the empty plates to the sink. His faded jeans curved over a rock-hard ass, and Sophie couldn't help but lick her lips. Then her gaze trailed over the crisp black shirt and the muscles shifting beneath it when he moved.

"You could probably get a job anywhere," she said.

His back stiffened as he ran water into the sink. "Probably."

"And make a lot of money." Her mind spun with the possibilities.

"More than likely." He placed the plates in the dishwasher

before turning to face her, his back against the counter, his arms across his chest. "I'm not leaving Montana."

Yeah, she'd been considering the thought. "Why not?"

"It's my heritage. I want Leila to grow up here and know her heritage. Be loved by her grandparents and uncles. Maybe cousins someday." His face hardened.

"You've had this discussion before," Sophie said softly.

Jake nodded.

"I like my life." She rose to her feet.

"Your life just changed. Both of ours did." Jake folded the dishtowel on the counter and put a hand to the small of her back. "Let's go to Doc's and make sure you're all right."

Sophie nodded. There really wasn't anything else to say. She followed him out of the house and climbed into his truck. They didn't speak on the way to the town center. All too soon Jake pulled to a stop near the spraying fountain, and Sophie turned toward a deep blue door set into a log-cabin-type building with *Doc Moon* written in yellow letters.

"There wasn't enough room for his whole name." Jake helped her from the Jeep.

Sophie sighed in relief at the mostly empty sidewalk before darting through the blue door into a comfortable mauve waiting room. The last thing she needed was the entire town knowing she was pregnant with Jake's baby.

"Well, hello, Jake." A fiftyish woman fluffed her poufed white hair and smiled capped teeth from behind the receptionist counter. "This must be Sophie. I'm Gladys, and I need you to fill these out." Gladys handed her a clipboard with several papers attached and a pen.

Sophie took them and dropped into a wooden chair. She had finished about half of the forms when a door to the right of the receptionist's desk opened.

Doc Mooncaller poked his gray head out. Today he wore an official-looking lab coat with a stethoscope draped over his neck. "Sophie, come on in. Just bring those papers." He moved back down the hall.

Sophie stood and wasn't surprised as Jake bounded up. She lifted an eyebrow at him.

His hopeful expression was too much to deny. "Can I come in?"

"Okay," she whispered, "but you have to leave if I need to get naked."

"I've seen you naked, Sunshine," he whispered back as they headed down the hall to the open examination room.

Sophie raised her arms in exasperation as she walked inside and plopped on one of the two brown guest chairs.

"Aren't you supposed to be on the table?" Jake sat next to her.

Sophie frowned. Suddenly, this was all too personal. "Maybe you should return to the waiting area."

"Too late," Jake whispered as Doc walked into the room.

"Well, Sophie. I guess you didn't make a run for it, huh?" Doc settled onto a rolling doctor's chair. "I'd like to do a full examination and medical history." He nodded toward the table. "My nurse will be in to give you a gown and take your blood pressure in just a minute. Jake, you go back to the waiting room."

Jake straightened. "But Doc—"

"I mean it. You can come next time. Right now you're just in the way," the doctor said.

"Fine. But if you need me, call me." Jake dropped a light kiss on Sophie's head before grudgingly leaving the room.

CHAPTER 19

*S*ophie walked down Doc's hall to the reception area, relieved he'd given her a clean bill of health. And prenatal vitamins. She took a deep breath and opened the door to face Jake. Then she stopped cold at the sight of Loni, Tom, Dawn, Colton, Quinn, and Hawk all sitting in the waiting room.

Jake held his head in his hands but looked up at her gasp. "Melanie Johnson saw us come into the office earlier and called Mrs. West, who called Jeanie Dixon, who called my mother."

Loni jumped to her feet and rushed to take Sophie's hands. "Are you okay?" Loni wore a light blue blouse with the buttons lined incorrectly, jeans, and mismatched flip-flops. Her hair perched in a lopsided ponytail, and she'd applied mascara to only one eye.

Sophie nodded numbly.

"Good." Loni patted her hands as the rest of the group rose. "We hurried down here so quickly we missed breakfast. Why don't we all—"

"No." Jake reached around Loni to take Sophie's hand and pull her toward the door. "We're going somewhere else. To talk."

He led her to the truck, and she sat inside without a protest, her mind whirling. She was pregnant. Everyone knew it. She didn't notice when he started the ignition or pulled onto the road, and she paid no attention to their trip. The truck stopped.

"You brought me to your house," she said woodenly.

Jake faced her across the middle console. "Are you all right?"

"Doc says I'm perfectly healthy. You had a huge head when you were born," she mused.

Jake laughed. "He told you that?"

"Everybody knows I'm pregnant." She would've liked a chance to come to grips with the idea on her own.

He rubbed a large hand over his eyes. "I know." He turned and unfolded from the truck before crossing and opening her door to help her out.

"Are you going to sue me for custody?" Sophie regained her footing on the smooth drive, then lifted her eyes to meet his, which narrowed. She fought a shiver as the pine-scented breeze rippled through her hair, and thunder sounded in the distance.

"No," he said.

Her knees trembled. "What about the Federal Indian Act?"

"You mean the Indian Child Welfare Act?" Jake rubbed heat into her suddenly freezing arms.

"Yeah, that." Sophie eased back from his too-appealing touch. "Don't tribes get a leg-up in custody battles?"

Jake studied her for a moment, realization dawning over his rugged face. "No. That is not what the Act does."

"Really?" Sarcasm laced her tone.

"The Act's purpose is to protect Indian children taken out of a home, so they are put in a foster home or adopted by another Indian couple. It does not give a leg-up to anyone in a normal custody proceeding." Jake propelled her toward the house. "I cannot believe you've actually been worrying about this." He opened the door and ushered her inside. "That you think I'd fight you in court for our child."

Sophie turned to face him as he shut the door with a soft *thud*. "What are you going to do?"

"Negotiate." The smile he gave her should have provided a warning. Instead, it warmed her from the toes up.

"Negotiate? What exactly do you mean?" Sophie sat on the leather couch and stretched her legs over the matching ottoman. The view of Mineral Lake and sharp peaked mountains relaxed her, bone by bone.

"Well, what would it take for you to live in Montana?" The matching leather chair creaked as he sat and faced her.

Sophie stiffened. "Live here?"

"Yes. In what circumstances can you see yourself based out of here?" he asked.

"What about you,? What circumstances can you see yourself living in San Francisco?" she asked.

"I don't." Jake's jaw set. "It's not only me. I can't take Leila away from the rest of my family. Even if I wanted to."

Sophie could understand that. "I'm surprised you're not spouting that we need to get married before the baby is born."

Jake sat back in his chair, his voice softening. "Already made that mistake."

Sophie clamped down on the sudden pang through her heart. She reminded herself she didn't want to get married just because she was pregnant, either. "I don't know where we stand."

"Me neither. I think we should look at it in steps," he said.

"In steps?"

Determination and an odd vulnerability lit his eyes. "The pregnancy as the first step. Sophie, I would not like to miss any of it."

"You'll come to San Francisco?" she asked.

"I thought you'd stay here. You know, work on the tribe's golf course and the art showing for Juliet. You'd still be working at what you want, and I'd pay to fly you to California any time you wished. So long as Doc okays it," Jake said.

The idea did sound appealing. "I'm not sure."

"Just think about it. Then we could figure out a schedule that works for both of us after the baby is born, if you decide to live in the city." His smile was too charming.

Sophie frowned, her mind reeling with static.

A slam of a truck door saved her from having to answer, and Leila opened the front door and rushed into the room. "Daddy, look what Aunt Dawn made me." The little girl jumped into her father's arms and handed him a blue knitted hat.

Jake raised his eyebrows. "Dawn learned to knit?"

"Uncle Hawk bet her that she couldn't do it." Leila turned curious eyes on Sophie. "What's 'knocked up' mean?"

Sophie's breath caught. She dropped her legs off the ottoman.

Jake shot her a concerned glance. "Where did you hear that, sweetheart?"

Dawn answered from the doorway. "That cow Betsy Phillips said it to Mary Whitmore at the grocery store when we dropped by for some flour for Mom." She turned wide eyes on Sophie. "Oh. Hi, Sophie."

Sophie leaned back again and crossed her arms over her face. "Hi, Dawn."

"Well, 'bye." Dawn made a quick exit.

"What's knocked up?" Leila asked again. "That cow Betsy Phillips said that you're knocked up, Sophie. Does it hurt?"

Sophie huffed out a laugh, and she peeked between her arms.

"You shouldn't call Mrs. Phillips a cow. Even if it is true," Jake admonished his daughter.

"Sorry." Inquisitive eyes met Sophie's. "Well?"

"Um, well." Sophie panicked as she stared at Jake.

Jake took a deep breath before cuddling his daughter close. "It means Sophie has a baby in her tummy."

"Like old Bula?" Leila's eyes dropped to Sophie's stomach.

Jake sputtered. "Uh, kind of."

"Who's Bula?" Sophie asked warily.

Jake coughed, obviously hiding a laugh. "A milk cow over at my mom's."

"How did you get a baby in your tummy?" Leila asked.

THAT NIGHT FOUND Sophie struggling to find sleep, even though her body was exhausted after Jake and Leila dropped her at home. She giggled at the thought of Jake quickly changing the subject to shoes with his daughter to avoid explaining the birds and the bees. Though they'd have to tell her about her future sibling sometime.

As much as she didn't want to admit it, Jake's offer made a certain kind of sense. Designing the tribe's course would help Uncle Nathan, and she'd get a chance to put together a real art exhibit. A dream she hadn't dared given any hope.

A tiny voice in her head whispered that she wouldn't be alone during the pregnancy, either. But instead of reassuring her, that made her want to run. Fast and hard in the other direction. The phone rang, and she reached for it like a lifeline.

"Hey, Sophie, I hope I'm not waking you," Preston said.

"No, Preston, I can't sleep," she admitted.

The sound of Preston settling back against leather, probably his desk chair, filled the line. "I just wanted to let you know that the Charleton Group has dropped their threats of a lawsuit."

Sophie's stomach heaved. "How? Why?"

"Apparently our new attorney talked to theirs and they backed off. Fast," Preston said.

Sophie groaned. "We have a new attorney?"

"Yeah. You might know him."

"Son of a bitch." Sophie took a calming breath. At this rate there wouldn't be a place in her life Jake hadn't infiltrated.

Preston laughed. "I figured I'd give you a friendly warning. Your uncle thinks Lodge walks on water."

"Great. But what about the other four developments? We needed those," she said, her head hurting.

"Nah, we'll be all right. I'm flying to New York tomorrow to meet with Luxem Hotel Executives. They're building seven more hotels next year, all with golf courses. I think we'll get the job," Preston said.

Hope filled her. "That'd be great."

"It'd be even better if you were here to help design some of those," he cajoled.

Sophie stared at muted moonlight playing across the ceiling and searched for the right words. The scraping of pine needles against the window was the only sound through the room.

"Or…" Preston's voice softened. "I'm sure you could help design them from anywhere in the world."

She breathed in. "Really?"

"All you need is the Internet and a cell phone," he said.

"I have those," Sophie said softly.

"You have me, too. You're a good friend. If you need me for anything, I'll be there," he said.

She kept her condition to herself for now. She wasn't ready to share. "Thanks."

"Night." Preston ended the call, and Sophie stretched to place the cell phone on the antique nightstand. It sounded like her old friend was saying good-bye. Curiosity at what might have been caught her before she rolled over to count sheep.

She reached the two hundredth white fluffy animal before an odd smell tickled her nose. She lifted her head to survey the air. Hazy beams of light filtered through the gauzy curtains and lent an ethereal glow to the old-fashioned room. Brass glinted off bedrails, and shadows hummed along the edges to settle into the corners.

The smell grew stronger.

Smoke. Oh God, it was smoke.

Gasping, Sophie jumped out of bed and leaned one hand on the night table as the world spun around her. Several deep breaths had the room righting itself so she could hurry to the door and pull it open. Smoke billowed up from the stairway. Flames licked the wooden handrail.

Panic shot through her.

She slammed the door closed and grabbed her sweatshirt off the flowered chair to cover the space under the door. Thank goodness Mrs. Shiller was out of town.

Sophie grabbed her cell and dialed 911 to report the fire before yanking on jeans, a sweater, and her boots. Then she ran to the window and pushed it all the way open before turning back to the room. The solid door kept too much smoke from entering, and she figured she had a few minutes to figure out the safest way down. The tree was the only option.

She threw out her suitcase and sketchbooks, watching them plummet two stories onto the thick grass, counting how long it took to hit the ground. Too long. She didn't know the exact distance, but she'd definitely break bones if she fell out of the tree. Smoke wafted out the front of the house to cover the ground in a fine haze.

From a distance, sirens pierced the night.

Sophie finally swung one leg over the ledge of the window. "We can do this, baby." She eyed the nearby thick branches of the statuesque bull pine. She'd never climbed a tree but had studied gravity in a physics class. Gravity would win over wishful hopes any day. She reached for the closest branch, her plan formulating as she moved.

Flashing blue and red lights stopped her mid-reach as the

sheriff's truck slammed to a stop and both Jake and Quinn jumped out. More shrill sirens sounded in the night.

"Sophie!" Jake yelled as he barreled across the grass to look up at the window, Quinn on his heels.

"I'm fine, Jake," Sophie called down, her white knuckles on the window frame starting to ache.

Quinn said something into a big radio just as a red fire truck screeched to a stop and men in full gear scrambled off.

Jake's eyes held Sophie's captive as he murmured something to his brother, who nodded and turned to direct the crew. Then Jake jogged to the tree and jumped to clasp the bottom branch before swinging his legs up over his head toward another branch, crossing his ankles and levering himself into the tree.

Sophie held her breath as Jake easily climbed branch after branch and sent leaves and bark cascading down to the ground.

Suddenly, he stood even with the window. "You ever climb a tree, Sunshine?"

CHAPTER 20

*S*ophie shook her head, tears surprising her as they cooled her face.

Scratches marred Jake's hands and bark wove through his hair. "Okay. You're going to reach out to that branch"—he pointed to the branch she had been aiming for—"and inch along until you get even with my hands." He nodded to the spot. "Then, when I touch your wrists, you get ready to move quickly, okay?" His voice stayed soft, soothing.

Sophie jumped as her bedroom door crackled into fire. Smoke filled the area behind her.

"Now," Jake coaxed as he shifted his weight on a straining branch.

Quinn took up a position directly below Sophie as she leaned forward and grasped the branch with both hands.

Following Jake's directions, she inched her hands and arms toward the trunk of the tree until her knees sat on the windowsill. She couldn't go any farther without putting all of her weight on the branch.

"Good job. Now this is a hundred-year-old tree, very sturdy, very safe. But that branch you're holding won't hold your entire weight for very long. Do you see the branch about three feet below it? The really thick one?" Jake pointed.

Smoke filled her nose, and she coughed, her eyes watering from the sting. "Yes."

"Good." Jake encircled both her wrists with his hands, balancing his weight while standing on two bowing branches. "So sweetheart," he said, speaking with confidence as more smoke spilled out from the window, "you need to grab this branch and swing your feet onto the lower one. It'll hold you all day. Ready?"

Sophie panicked and tried to pull her hands back.

Jake shook his head. "The fire's behind you, Soph. You have to move—now."

"It's okay," Quinn called up from the ground. "I'm right under you. If worse comes to worse, you'll land on me."

Jake tightened his grip as the firemen slammed through the front door armed with axes and an uncoiled hose. "Now, Sophie."

"Jake, the baby." Sophie clenched the branch with a quick look down. Way down to where Quinn stood patiently.

"Babies don't like smoke." Jake's voice lowered. "Besides, ours would love to flatten Uncle Quinn, I'm sure."

Sophie tried to breathe shallowly and not take in too much smoke. With a quick prayer, she seized the branch and swung from the safety of the window, her heart all but beating out of her rib cage.

Her feet hit the lower branch and slipped off, her boots scraping for purchase.

Panic squashed the breath from her lungs.

Sophie cried out as her legs dangled, and the sound of a branch snapping in two filled the air. It disintegrated in clumps of bark between her hands. Jake's hands tightened on her wrists as he held her in midair before he swung her so her feet could again find purchase. She caught the lower branch and pressed her legs forward until her feet balanced on it.

She stood for a second, her feet on the branch, her wrists in Jake's broad hands, before he tugged her toward the trunk and wrapped her arms around the tree.

Sophie rested her head against the scratchy bark and her knees began to tremble.

"Okay, almost done now," Jake whispered into her ear as he positioned his body behind hers. "See that branch to the right, about a foot down from you?"

Sophie twisted her head to look. "Yes."

"Hold onto the trunk and just step one foot down." Jake pressed even closer. "I've got you, I promise."

Sophie stepped down, her palms scraping the bark as she fought for balance. Then she sighed in relief as she lowered her other foot. The crackle of fire and shattering glass boomed around them. The process continued until they both stood on bottom branches, about seven feet from the ground. At Jake's quiet order, Sophie sat, her hands gripping the trunk while he jumped to the grass.

"Grab my arms and jump." Jake reached up with both hands.

Sophie reached down, clasped his broad arms, and let gravity have its way. Her feet met wet grass for a mere second before Jake scooped her in his arms and strode for the paramedic van on the street.

Sophie coughed lightly into his neck, her stomach heaving as Jake lowered her on the tailgate of his truck and a uniformed paramedic placed oxygen over her nose and mouth. Thunder crackled in the distance, and a light rain peppered the ground. Jake pushed Sophie farther into the back of the truck, into dryness.

She closed her eyes and breathed deeply, the scratches on her hands searing. Red and blue lights swirled as the firefighters rolled up their hose and the stench of burned wood filled the air. She began to shake violently, her teeth chattering behind the mask.

"The fire's out," Jake said, his eyes on Quinn and a sooty fire-fighter as they surveyed the damage from the porch. He shifted so he stood directly between the smoldering walls and Sophie, and she wondered if it were intentional or instinctive. "How are you feeling?"

"Better. I don't think I inhaled much of the smoke. The baby should be fine," she gasped.

Jake didn't turn as he spoke. "I was worried about you."

"How did you get here so fast?" she asked.

Jake straightened as his brother approached. "Poker night at Hawk's. I was there when Quinn got the call."

"The fire was intentional." Quinn didn't waste any words as he reached Jake and cast a concerned gaze toward Sophie. "Most people know Mrs. Shiller is out of town."

"You sure?" Jake lowered his voice.

"Yes. Typical Molotov cocktail through the front window." Both men turned to study her—twin sets of deep onyx eyes with different expressions. Quinn was all cop, curious and hard. Jake's expression spoke of something dark, something heated.

Yet one thing remained the same—both were pissed.

"What?" Sophie scooted to the edge of the vehicle, letting rain splatter against her legs. "You think this was on purpose?"

Quinn nodded. "I know it was. Have you noticed anything odd, anyone following you while you've been here?"

"I haven't seen anyone following me. But…" She took a deep breath. "Somebody has left notes on the Jeep window for me."

Quinn placed a restraining hand on his brother's arm as Jake's eyes narrowed dangerously. "Notes?" he asked.

"Um, yeah. Basically saying that the development was a bad idea," she said.

"And?" Jake growled it.

The notes had seemed silly and not threatening. "That I

should get out of town," she said. "I planned to tell you about it but everything has been so busy. The notes were more goofy than scary. Well, mostly."

Jake swore under his breath while Quinn cast a glance at the milling spectators on the street and nearby lawns.

"I don't understand, I mean, the commissioners denied the application." Sophie's temper stirred. "There won't be a golf course."

Quinn shook his head. "The tribe has hired you to build a golf course."

Sophie shrugged, wary of the fury on Jake's face. This wasn't her fault. She turned her attention to Quinn. "I still have the notes. They're over in the suitcase I threw out the window." The muscle ticking in Jake's sooty jaw captured her gaze.

"Stay with her, Jake. Let me do my job." Quinn stepped around his brother and headed for the still smoldering house.

"I want to see them," Jake called to Quinn's retreating back.

"I know," Quinn tossed back over his shoulder, his legs eating the distance to the pile under the bull pine.

Jake's eyes bored holes in her as his arms slowly crossed over his broad chest.

"I didn't think it was a big deal." Sophie answered his unasked question, snapping the words out.

The muscle in his jaw swelled. "How many notes?"

"Three," she admitted.

"When?" he snapped.

Sophie was saved from answering when Quinn returned with her suitcase in one hand, the other pulling papers from beneath his jacket. Two dark, masculine heads dipped to read the notes in the muted light of the paramedic's vehicle. Sophie shivered at the looks on their faces once they finished reading.

Quinn nodded at her. "Get her home. I'll follow up with questions in the morning."

Jake reached for her.

"No." Sophie moved farther into the vehicle as lightning ripped across the sky.

Jake hauled her out of the rig and carried her to his truck, where a deputy finished loading her possessions into the back-seat. Jake opened his door and lifted her easily across the console before taking his own seat. He shut the door with more force than necessary. "You're coming with me."

"Damn it, Jake." Sophie fought the urge to kick him. Hard.

Jake didn't reply as he started the ignition and pulled past the emergency vehicles onto the rain-drenched road. Sophie pouted in her seat, determined to ignore him. He drove several miles in silence before speaking. "If you weren't pregnant, you'd absolutely be wearing my handprint on your ass right now."

Her butt actually clenched. "Good thing you knocked me up, then."

His dark gaze set a fluttering in her stomach. "Remind me to Google if spanking will hurt a pregnant woman."

"You don't scare me." Which was a complete freakin' lie. The guy was kind of scary...but he'd never hurt her.

"Why didn't you tell me about the notes?" he asked.

"They weren't really threats," Sophie huffed back.

"So it wasn't a big deal." Sarcasm wove through his every word.

Her arms crossed over her chest as she watched the storm wage outside the truck. "Right. Frankly, I didn't even think to tell you."

"Really," he drawled.

"Yes, really." Heat rose to her face. "This was just a quick fling, remember? A couple of weeks, then I was gone. Out of your life."

As they reached his home, Jake slammed the truck into park and turned off the ignition with a sharp twist of his wrist. "Once you discovered you were pregnant? You didn't think to let me know someone was threatening you?"

Sophie jumped out of the truck and headed for the house. She called over her shoulder, "They weren't threats." Yeah, she felt foolish for not reporting them to Quinn. No way would she admit it.

Jake followed close behind her, his long strides putting her between him and the house. He pulled her to a stop, a feral glimmer in his eyes. "You should have told me."

The fury of the storm was no match for the tempest rising inside her. "I didn't think to tell you. This was never going to be permanent."

"It is now," he said.

The rain smashed her hair against her face. "Wrong. We're exactly like this storm, Jake. Fiery, hot, even crazy. But you know what? You know the problem with sizzling summer storms?"

"No, what?" Even through the rain, his voice carried the hint of danger. Of wildness that outdid Mother Nature.

"They blow over. You settle back to enjoy the lightning show, the clap of thunder, and poof, they're gone." She yelled above the rising wind. "Blue sky follows along meekly, too quickly."

His white shirt plastered against tanned muscle. "We can't have blue sky?"

"Us? No way." The wind almost toppled her over. "You need to let me go, Jake."

The wind whipped his hair around his face, giving him a formidable, almost primitive look. His ancestry blazed in full force as he stood tall and firm against the gale. "Let you go? I think that's your fucking problem, Sophie."

"Meaning?" Her boots sunk into the mud as she struggled to keep her footing.

"Too many people have let you go." A quick swoop and she was in his arms, struggling against him with all her might as his strong body blocked the driving wind. "Your father, the bastard, left you. The second your mother married, she dumped you in some school. Didn't she?"

Sophie's battle against the strong arms shielding her from the wind was in vain.

"Even Preston. Mr. Golden Boy with the Rolex. He left you here for me," Jake said grimly.

She fought a shiver at the warm breath against her ear.

One broad boot kicked the door open. He dropped her to her feet and slammed the door against the storm, and his furious face lowered to within an inch of hers. "I'm not letting you go. What's more, you don't want me to." Male outrage blazed through his eyes.

They stood staring at each other, dripping rain onto the stone floor and panting in uneven breaths.

"You are overbearing," Sophie gritted out, fighting a shiver, fighting exhaustion.

"You're an independent pain in the ass." Jake ran a frustrated hand through his sopping hair, obviously trying to control his temper. He took a deep breath.

She glared at him.

His voice softened. "One who has been through an ordeal and needs a hot shower and a comfortable bed." He held out a hand. "Truce? At least for the night?" His words contrasted with the hard glint in his eye. He was raring for a fight.

Sophie slowly took his hand, her energy gone. She wasn't up to a fight. At least not right now. "All right. Just for the night."

CHAPTER 21

The low hum of male voices awoke Sophie the next morning. The night was a blur. She had taken a shower and then fallen asleep in Jake's big bed before her head even hit the pillow. With a moan, she snuggled deeper into the bed and tried to go back to sleep.

"It's time to get up." Jake suddenly filled the doorway. "I know you're awake."

"No." The pillow muffled her voice.

Jake moved into the room. "Yes."

"I need sleep," she mumbled, her eyes still closed.

"It seems we've had this discussion before." Jake chuckled. "Quinn is here and has questions for you. Get dressed and come on out."

Sophie groaned.

"Unless you want him to interview you in here," Jake offered.

Sophie glared through one slightly opened eyelid. "Fine. Just give me a minute."

"I will. Get up, sweetheart. We have a lot to talk about." He retraced his steps out of the room.

Sophie opened both eyes to see muted tones of navy and tan

and sensual paintings. Her possessions perched against the far wall. Jake must've brought them in earlier. She rolled herself to a sitting position before gingerly standing. The room spun and then settled. She headed for the attached bath.

A warm shower brought some life to her limbs, and she felt marginally better after dressing in comfortable jeans and her favorite green T-shirt. She yanked her curls into a ponytail and ran pink gloss over her lips before heading out to face the men waiting for her. All three of them.

They sat in the breakfast nook in faded jeans and long-sleeved T-shirts, thick mugs of steaming coffee on the oak table. The sliding glass door framed thick black clouds rumbling across a grumpy sky. Mineral Lake sat dark and still, waiting to get pummeled. Colton twirled leather gloves in his hand, his gaze idly following a tree branch slamming against the house. Quinn stopped whatever he'd been saying.

"Morning." Jake rose and grabbed a red mug off the counter to hand her, and then gestured her onto the seat next to him. Congeniality softened his tone, but his eyes were granite hard. The thick fragrance of Colombian beans greeted her. She sniffed appreciatively as she sat, ignoring the set of Jake's jaw.

"It's decaf," Quinn muttered with a glare at his own cup.

"I told you I wasn't making two pots." Jake reclaimed his seat.

Sophie took a small sip and warmth filled her. "You three look like you're heading out to work the ranch."

"We are." Jake nodded toward the tumultuous clouds. "We have repairs to make all over the ranch, at least before the next storm hits—which should be late tonight or early tomorrow morning."

"How's Mrs. Shiller's house?" Sophie asked Quinn.

Quinn shrugged. "I went by this morning and met with the fire marshal. The damage isn't as extensive as we thought last night. The living room and stairwell sustained both fire and smoke damage, the kitchen just some smoke. We haven't been able to track down Mrs. Shiller or Lily Roundtree yet, but they'll check in with Lily's niece one of these days. We have repairmen there already."

"Any news on the notes?" she asked and Jake stiffened.

"No. Your prints were the only ones on the paper. The handwriting isn't familiar." Quinn shook his head. "There are a lot of people who don't want any development in the area. The tribe faced organized opposition when we built the casino even though we're autonomous on our own land." He rubbed his chin. "Though this seems like just one individual."

Jake rolled his neck as if tension lived there. "So was the Unabomber. My money's on the Concerned Citizens Group."

"Maybe," Quinn allowed. "I'll head out tomorrow and talk to Billy Johnson."

"Rockefeller," Sophie said. Had her bout with the ketchup pissed off Billy enough that he'd try to kill her?

Quinn leaned forward. "Have you remembered anything? Noticed any strange cars around the neighborhood? Or any people walking or jogging down the street?"

Sophie shook her head. "I haven't noticed anything out of the ordinary."

"That's what I figured. I have deputies going door to door in Shiller's neighborhood. Maybe somebody saw something." Quinn took another drink of the unleaded brew and grimaced.

Silence sat comfortably around them until Colton pushed back from the table, his chair scraping across the thick wood floor. "Come on, Quinn. Let's saddle the horses. I want to get this done before I head back to school." He nodded to Jake. "We'll meet you at the barn." He dropped a quick kiss on Sophie's head and left.

Quinn unfolded himself to his feet and placed a reassuring hand on her shoulder when he passed her. "We'll find who started the fire. You'll be safe here today. Just stay close, all right?" He gave her a gentle squeeze before following Colton out of the room.

"Will you be all right here for a few hours?" Jake leaned forward and took one of her hands in his.

Sophie nodded, his broad hand warming her more than the coffee, his dark eyes smiling at her. "I'll be fine. I thought I'd try out the studio today. I mean, since your mom and Leila went to so much trouble."

A dimple twinkled from his pleased grin. "Do you need help with that?"

"No, and I'm not promising to stay."

"I know." He stood. "We need to talk, but right now I have to go make sure the steers are safely contained."

She wrapped both hands around the warm cup. "It's a nice space to paint, and I may do the exhibit for Juliet."

"No pressure." One knuckle under her chin tipped her face up for his lips to brush hers.

"Right," she murmured with a raised eyebrow as he chuckled and moved across the kitchen.

"I'm not sure how long we'll be, but you call me if you need me. I'll have my cell," he said.

Sophie nodded as he left the kitchen and turned back toward her coffee. The house fire had been meant for her. To harm or just scare, she wasn't sure. Now she was staying at Jake's, right where he wanted her.

Maybe she should fly back to California for some perspective. But the canvases and oil paints beckoned her from the bedroom. It wouldn't hurt to at least see how well the studio worked. She could start one painting, since her day was free. It didn't mean she was moving to Montana for any length of time.

Reassured, she finished her coffee before dodging into the bedroom where she pulled on a pale sweatshirt, gathered the few art supplies that still had been in her suitcase, and darted out the front door. Her hair blew around her face as she ran toward the garage, climbed the wooden steps to the landing, and pushed open the door. Dim light cut through sparkling dust mites as she slammed the door with one booted foot. The room was as perfect as she remembered.

Smiling, she glanced out the wide southern window to the storm lurking just over the lake. The urge to paint the scene bubbled through her veins, and she set up her easel and settled a pristine white canvas in place. She spread oils onto a board, chose the correct brush, and started to paint the mood.

Several hours later, she made herself dinner in the main house. The storm had held itself at bay the entire day, almost as if it posed over the lake just to assist in her brush strokes. The phone rang as she finished stirring an aromatic beef stew in a Crock-Pot for Jake, who'd called earlier and hoped to be back soon. She answered, figuring it'd be okay with him.

"Hi, Sophie, it's Rachel from the general store. The delivery guy just dropped off your new charcoals. I'm sorry the old ones burned up in the fire."

Sophie fought to keep from asking why the petite teenager had known to call her at Jake's. There weren't many secrets in the small town. "How late are you open today?"

"About another hour; we want to miss the storm," Rachel said.

Sophie chewed on her lip gloss. "You think we have an hour until it arrives?"

"Definitely, but no longer than an hour," Rachel said.

Perfect. "Okay, I'll be right there." Sophie cast a wary glance upward and then grabbed her keys and ran to the Jeep. It'd be at least an hour, maybe more, before the storm arrived, and she needed the charcoals to sketch out her paintings for the next day.

Nobody knew where she was today, so she felt safe enough to make the quick trip.

The storm held off as she drove the fifteen miles to the

general store across from Doc Mooncaller's. She parked, dodged inside, and paid Rachel for the box of charcoals just as the girl was shutting down the lights for the day.

Fat raindrops began to fall as she pulled into the street to head back to Jake's, her new supplies perched safely on the backseat. The passenger door flew open and a lanky teenager leaped inside. Sophie jumped and slammed the brakes.

"Sorry if I scared you." He turned sorrow-filled brown eyes her way.

Fear caught the breath in her throat. "I know you. You were in the crowd at the Concerned Citizens meeting." Sophie eased the Jeep to the side of the road. The slam of drops on metal drowned out the sound of the running engine.

The kid nodded his blond buzz-cut head, his slender hands running along his dark jeans before he wiped his nose on the back of one sleeve. "I'm Jeremy." He had to be fourteen, maybe fifteen.

For some reason, she felt calm. "Hi."

"Jeremy Rockefeller."

"Ah," she murmured.

"I, um…" A deep red blush stole across his features. "I wanted to apologize. For the fire."

Her heart clutched. "*You* set the fire?"

"Yeah. I didn't know you were pregnant." His eyes filled with tears.

Sophie whirled on the boy. "What difference does that make? It was okay to kill me otherwise?" Fury lit her tone and she stifled the urge to shake the kid.

"Kill you?" Jeremy vehemently shook his head. "Jeez, lady, I wasn't trying to kill you. Mrs. Shiller was out of town, and you had that big tree right outside your window. I knew you'd be all right. Everyone can climb a tree."

Oh. That probably did make sense to a kid. "What were you trying to do?" she asked.

"Be a man. Stand up for what was right." He wiped the back of a hand across his eyes.

"By leaving scary notes and firebombing an old woman's house?" Sophie's voice shook.

His shoulders drooped even more. "Dumb. I know. But your development would've raped the land. I just wanted to do something. For once."

Sophie softened. The kid's misery was obvious. It certainly couldn't be easy being raised by the odd Rockefeller couple. "So why confess?"

"I can't sleep. I can't eat. I just feel so bad." His words rang true.

Sophie's thoughts reeled. The kid was obviously scared. And remorseful. But this wasn't her decision to make. "We have to tell the sheriff."

"I know." Sniff.

She'd been a scared kid with crappy parents at one time, too. "If you promise to channel your aggression better and work for Mrs. Shiller one day a week for the next year, I won't press charges."

"Really?" Hope filled the brown depths of his eyes.

"Really, but I can't guarantee Mrs. Shiller will agree and not press charges, and I don't know what the sheriff will do." She really didn't want to know what Quinn would do.

Jeremy held out a skinny hand and they shook. "It's a deal, anyway."

"Okay." Sophie pulled back onto the road and circled around the fountain to the sheriff's office. Quinn met them at the curb, probably having seen them from his window. Rain curled through his thick black hair and plastered his denim shirt and faded jeans against his body.

Quinn's eyes revealed nothing as Jeremy slowly exited the vehicle. "Are you okay, Soph?"

"I'm fine. Jeremy has a confession to make, and I don't want to press charges," Sophie said.

Quinn's eyes hardened on the boy as he slammed the car door. He rapped three knuckles against the window and waited until she rolled it down a bit. "I'll need a statement from you."

"Nope. I have nothing to say. It's over as far as I'm concerned," she said.

Quinn shook his head. "Jake might have something to say about that."

Sophie shrugged. "It's not up to Jake. It's my decision and I've made it."

Quinn's lips twisted in almost a smile.

"What?" she asked.

"Just glad Jake is the brother who captured you. That's all."

"Funny. Say hi to Juliet for me." With her parting shot, she rolled up the window, gave Jeremy a reassuring nod, and pulled back onto the street. Jeremy, a pitiful expression on his face, watched her drive away. She accelerated and made quick work of the road back to Jake's. Her cell phone rang just as his home came into view.

"Where are you?" Jake's voice barely wove through the crackle.

She fought the urge to snap. Darn meddling Lodge men. "I suppose you talked to your brother?"

"You should press charges," Jake said.

She rolled her eyes. "No. It's my choice."

"Fine. Where are you, softy?" he asked.

"Pulling into the drive," she said, stopping the vehicle.

She clicked off as the front door opened to reveal him, long and lean in the doorway. The sight of him, tall and sexy and waiting for her, tightened her chest as she jumped out of the Jeep, her charcoals safe in her hands. Jake took them from her as he pulled her inside, out of the misting rain.

"There's a storm coming." Warm arms enveloped her as the scent of horse, dust, and man surrounded her.

"You need a shower." She wrinkled her nose while stepping back.

Jake kept his gaze on her as he gently placed her box by the door. "Sounds like an offer."

"What—" was all she got out before two strong arms whisked her up and carried her toward the master bedroom. "Why are you always carrying me?"

Jake dropped his mouth to nibble along her jawline. Straight to the shell of her ear. "I like you in my arms."

"You like being in control." Breathiness coated her words, and she tilted her head so he had better access.

"I like you safe in my sights. And here"—he tightened his arms, his sizzling mouth now exploring her neck—"is the perfect way to do both." He lowered her to the bathroom tile. Two rough hands lifted her shirt over her head. His gaze hot on her, he yanked his shirt off before his hands unclasped her bra. It fell into the growing heap of clothing as he unsnapped his dusty jeans. He pushed them down muscled thighs along with his shorts, his eyes warming as she kicked off her boots and shimmied out of her pants.

"Rough day, cowboy?" She nodded to a deep purple bruise across one thick bicep.

He twisted the shower knob. "My mind wasn't on the job at hand." Steam began filling the air.

"What was your mind on?" she asked.

"This." One long tapered finger traced her collarbone and explored south to the peak of one pebbled nipple.

"Oh." Heat filled her.

He stepped forward and backed her into the stone tiled alcove. "And this." Two strong hands went to her buttocks and lifted her against the smooth tile. His mouth dropped to hers, gentle and sweet. The spray beat against his back and cascaded around to mist her.

Sophie wrapped both hands around his neck and both legs around his hips. "And this." His hand slid around to press ever so softly above her left breast. "I want your heart." His mouth dipped to replace his hand. "You already have mine. When I think about that kid jumping in the car with you..."

"He was just a scared kid. Not dangerous." Did Jake just say he wanted her heart? That silly organ fluttered hard.

"You wouldn't know dangerous if it bit you." To prove his point, he bit down into sensitive flesh.

Sophie gasped as sharp pangs of desire shot directly south. "Jake..." Her head fell back as his mouth moved down and engulfed her nipple in heat.

"I told you I'd never lie to you." His rumble against her flesh shot spasms deep within her. "I meant it when I said I was keeping you."

Her hands moved to the powerful strength of his dark chest and down the arms holding her securely, before moving back up to clench in his hair and yank his head to meet hers. Her legs tightened around him as she deepened the kiss. His tongue swept her mouth, one hand cupping the back of her head, the other squeezing her buttocks.

She pressed harder into him. "Now, Jake," she moaned against his mouth.

With a quick movement, he impaled her against the wall and joined them together.

"Jake." It was too much. Sophie clenched his shoulders and tilted her head against the wall. Jake nuzzled his lips along her neck, keeping them both in place, on the edge of something.

Something amazing.

She swallowed as a tremor shook her. "Have you noticed you always have me against a wall?" she breathed.

"This is the perfect position for you." His hands tightened.

She sucked in air, her sex throbbing. Electricity rushed through her veins. Her nerves sparked. "We do seem to fit."

He lifted his head, dark eyes devouring her. "I didn't like you out in that storm."

"I beat the storm home." Her eyes focused on his talented lips. His eyes heated even more. She opened her mouth to qualify the term *home*, only to have Jake swoop in and stop the words in her throat. Unapologetically. He kissed her until her mind reeled, until her heart turned over in her chest, and until she began to move against him, her feet pressing his buttocks with fervor.

Finally, Jake lifted his head and pulled torturously out of her before slamming back inside with a twist of his hips, his eyes focused on hers. Sophie clutched his shoulders. A stirring started deep inside her. Jake did it again.

"Promise me you won't go out in a storm like that again." His husky voice wrapped around her with the steam.

"Are you kidding me?" She groaned and struggled to move.

"Deadly serious." And he was. The muscled arms holding her vibrated with the need to move. A fierce muscle ticked in his jaw. His eyes hardened to obsidian sparks. His expression showed he'd wait all day for an answer.

Oh, she'd gotten by just fine. "I'll avoid driving in storms." She would've promised just about anything to get him moving again. Quick as a flip of a switch, Jake gripped her buttocks and moved, all strength, speed, and muscle.

She trembled. A tightening in her abdomen compressed her lungs. Tingles of erotic shards rippled up her legs and over her thighs.

She ran her hands over his shoulders to the shifting deltoid muscles. So much strength in such an intelligent man. Throw in the inherent dominance that made her see stars, and every ounce of determination she owned spiraled into wanting to keep him. Forever.

He thrust harder, angling his pelvis to brush her clit.

She gasped, her hold tightening. Painfully hard nipples brushed his chest, sending sparks of fire to her sex. To her already engorged, ready to explode, aching clit.

Her hands explored farther over solid muscle and deep hollows to reach his vibrating biceps. He was so strong. He could do anything he wanted to her. The thought heated her, and the knowledge that he wanted to take her completely almost sent her over the edge.

His cock stretched her, electrifying her nerve endings as he pounded.

She ground against him, climbing higher, seeking that detonation only Jake could provide. He hammered into her, gripping her hip with one hand, his fingers on the other cupping her head.

A twister whirled through her. She broke. Nerves flared, and waves rippled through her so brutally she cried out. Holding tight, her body rigid, she clung to Jake to keep her safe.

The prolonged climax tore her world apart, and she whispered his name.

CHAPTER 22

*S*everal hours after playing in the shower with Jake, eating the delicious stew while arguing over poor Jeremy's fate, and making love again in the big bed, Sophie dropped into an exhausted sleep.

She had odd dreams about skiing through storms all night, and awoke with a start, her eyes adjusting to early morning light filtering through the shades. She rolled over and buried her face into Jake's vacated pillow, filling her senses with the scent of man and musk. Hmm. His pillow was still warm. She snuggled closer and opened one eye on the empty doorway, her mind awakening much faster than her body.

What a night. Jake had been there for her, in her life, every step of the way. When she'd been confronted by the Citizen's Group, when she'd needed to climb away from a fire, even when she'd been lost and confused. He was a man who stuck.

She'd always wanted that kind of security. And love.

The thought hit her square in the chest. She loved the man. Completely.

Did he love her? She squared her shoulders. Forget things

working out. As a smart woman, as a strong one, she'd make sure things worked out. Whether Jake Lodge liked it or not.

She rolled out of bed with a smile on her face, yanked on jeans and a cream sweater, then padded barefoot into the kitchen. The echo of a clock filled the room as her gaze fell onto a note on the black marble counter.

Morning, Sunshine. There's decaf in the cupboard above the coffeepot. I've gone to meet Colton in the south pasture—steers loose and fence down from the last storm. There's another one coming, so stay inside. Love, Jake

P.S. About the storm, you're mistaken. We'll never blow over.

Sophie noted the signature, and her heart hummed. He used the *L* word. Maybe he actually meant it.

Thunder pealed directly overhead, and a slash of lightning lit the cheery kitchen. Her stomach rumbled, and her head began to ache. "All right, baby, let's get some food." She filed through the shelves of the pantry. Ah, saltine crackers. Wonderful. A quick look into the fridge discovered butter and strawberry jam, homemade by Loni. The perfect combination.

Sophie placed her treats on the island and munched quietly, her gaze fixed on the dark clouds rolling toward her over the mountains. She finished her plate and looked through the fridge, still hungry. At this point she'd weigh a ton by the time the baby was born. Oooh, cold macaroni salad. Probably Loni's. Sophie took the bowl to the island to eat, enjoying the storm. Lightning jagged across the sky, and she jumped. The lights flickered.

A phone jarred her from her thoughts. Jake's landline. What if it was Colton? No. He would've called Jake's cell. Sophie let it ring, listening intently when Jake's deep voice on the machine told the caller to leave a message.

"Jake?" Hysterics lifted Dawn's voice. "You're not picking up your cell..." Static came over the line. "But...storm...road... there's...blood. I need help."

Sophie lost the rest of the woman's words. She jumped for the phone. "Dawn? Where are you? Dawn?"

"Sophie? I'm...bottom...of Jake's hill... Call Jake. There's blood. Need help." The phone went dead.

"Dawn? Dawn, answer me," Sophie yelled into the phone. A drumming buzz met her ear. She hung up the phone then grabbed it again and dialed Jake's cell. It went directly to voice mail. What to do? Sophie paced the cozy kitchen. "Okay. Dawn's in trouble. At the bottom of Jake's. Jake's what? The drive?" The drive was several miles long. Perhaps she'd slid off the road below. Sophie jumped at a loud thunderclap. She couldn't leave Dawn at the bottom of the hill. If that's where she was.

Sophie ran into the living room and grabbed a thick flannel jacket out of the closet. "It's okay, baby," she whispered as she buttoned it and rolled the sleeves up to free her hands. "We'll get Dawn and come right back. No problem." She wondered if the baby could hear the rapid beating of her heart. Then she wondered if the baby could even hear yet. Probably not.

After yanking on her boots, she ran into the rain, slipping once in the thickening mud and dropping to one knee. Her jeans shredded, and her skin smarted as blood began to well. With a hiss of frustration, she pushed to her feet and bolted for the rented Jeep, her pant leg stiff with mud and blood. She jumped inside the car, fastened her seat belt, wiped the rain from her face, and started carefully down the drive.

Wind slashed at the vehicle, pushing it to one side of the road where branches scraped the side like fingernails against a chalkboard. Water ran in rivulets across the dark asphalt, throwing the vehicle into a slide.

Sophie gingerly pumped the brakes. "This is bad," she whispered while jerking the wheel to the left. Rain beat against the windshield so hard even the fastest wiper setting failed to clear the view. Lightning crackled across the sky. Sophie yelped as a fallen branch clattered on the hood.

She slammed on the brakes and panted. Maybe this wasn't such a good idea.

"I already know this isn't a good idea," she muttered to the empty vehicle. "But Dawn needs help, and we can make it." No way could she leave Jake's sister hurt and scared at the bottom of the drive.

She pressed on the accelerator while twisting the heat controls to defog the windows. There, that was better.

The road stretched down the hill, empty save for falling pinecones and branches. The wind battered the vehicle like a boxer without his gloves, hard, merciless, dirty. Sophie struggled to keep the Jeep stable on the roadway. The wind shifted, and rain angled straight at her. The cascading heat from the vents failed to warm her chilled bones. Her knuckles white on the wheel, she ventured farther down the road.

She made it about a mile before lightning snapped right in front of her. The crash of a splintering tree roared over the rain. With a cry, Sophie yanked the wheel to the left to avoid the falling white pine, sending the car hydroplaning across the asphalt. A loud crunch of buckling metal rose over the fury of the storm. She shut her eyes as the vehicle bounced twice, spun to the side, and rolled.

Darkness swirled as she fell unconscious.

SOPHIE AWOKE to rain drumming against metal and pain screaming through her head. She tried to move, opening her eyes and realizing she was upside down. "Oh," she moaned, reaching for her seat belt and pushing the button with trembling hands. She dropped onto her already aching head, her breath whooshed out, and she curled into a fetal position on the inside of the roof.

The Jeep teetered upside down, and branches covered the

shattered windshield and blocked her view. Groaning, she leaned forward and tried to open the driver's side door but it wouldn't budge. "Okay," she whispered. "It's okay. I'm okay." She wiped tears and blood off her face and curled into a ball around the baby. "Jake will come."

She pushed the deflated airbag out of her way and concentrated on her body. Her head hurt, and everything else ached. The ignition had turned off, so she didn't have to worry about that. The metal protested beneath her as she shuffled into a more comfortable position. Where was Jake?

Tears filled her eyes as her stomach cramped.

The baby.

She couldn't lose the baby. Until that moment she hadn't realized how badly she wanted the little one. And Jake. She finally had a chance for a real family, for a man who wouldn't leave her. She loved him. She'd known it for a while. As nausea spiraled through her and darkness crept across her vision, she wondered if it was too late.

CHAPTER 23

The pelting rain, the swirling sirens, the crumpled metal—Jake had been here before. The devastating *déjà vu* of the moment froze his legs in place.

Through the smashed window, the limp body of the woman he loved failed to move. Devastating pain shot through him at the thought of losing her. His chest actually pounded in agony.

Fire lit through him. Not again. He wouldn't lose Sophie.

He jumped toward the upside-down vehicle and grabbed the door handle.

Strong arms banded around him and twisted to the side. Fury leaped through his veins, more powerful than any storm. He pivoted and shoved Quinn. Hard.

His brother slipped in the mud. He growled and pounced, both hands grabbing Jake's arms. "Stop it."

Jake was beyond reason. Only one thing mattered—getting to Sophie. The primitive being deep within him surged to the surface. He shrugged from his brother's grasp and rushed toward the vehicle, shoving a paramedic out of the way.

The tackle from behind dropped him into the mud and away from the car.

Rage heated every neuron in his body. He flipped around, both hands clapping Quinn's face.

Quinn howled in anger and punched him in the jaw. "Fucking knock it off. The car isn't stable—we need to go in through the other side." For good measure, he punched him again. "Let us do our job."

Jake blinked. Reality returned. Mud squished his back, and his heavy-as-hell brother flattened him to the ground. He stared into his brother's concerned eyes. "She left me."

Quinn yanked them both to their feet. "She didn't leave you —not Sophie. This is different."

Maybe. Jake turned toward the car. "I need to know. Is she—"

"I don't know." Quinn shoved him. "Stay here. I'll check."

Jake nodded, helplessness catching in his throat. She couldn't be dead.

He kept his gaze on his brother as he maneuvered around the firefighters trying to open Sophie's door. Quinn leaned in and then slowly stepped back. "She's alive."

Jake hit his knees. Thank God.

Then he leaped forward to tear the car apart and get her out.

※　※　※

SOPHIE OPENED her eyes slowly to a white wall and bright lights. A dull pounding set up in her skull, so she turned her head to where Jake slumped in a chair, his chin on his chest, his hair wet under a black cowboy hat, his shirt and jeans streaked with mud. She shifted to the right.

Loni moved forward in her chair, her black eyes bright with concern, her hair a lopsided mess atop her head.

"My baby?" Sophie croaked, her throat on fire.

"The baby's fine." Loni reached and smoothed back Sophie's curls.

The pain receded to a dull roar as other aches and pains sprang to life. "Dawnie?" Sophie asked.

Loni nodded. "Dawn is fine. Hawk found her at the bottom of the hill. She wrecked her car but only had a couple of small cuts and plenty of bruises. Dawn was more scared than hurt. They're waiting the storm out at Hawk's place."

Sophie glanced over at Jake. "I wasn't running away from him." Tears filled her eyes.

"I know. Though you should probably tell him that, sweetheart." Loni nodded toward the midnight dark gaze running over her face. So Jake had awakened. "I'm going to go call Colton. He's worried sick." She hurried from the room.

Sophie's throat felt like sandpaper as she turned toward Jake. "I thought you were asleep."

"I was praying," Jake said.

"I wasn't running away from you," she whispered.

His chair creaked as he leaned forward and gently clasped one of her hands in his. Raw cuts and bruises welled from his knuckles. "I know. What were you doing?"

She gasped at his hurt.

A purpling bruise spread along his jaw. "The Jeep's metal put up a fight while we were getting you out," he confirmed. He stroked his finger down her cheek. "Where were you going in that storm?"

"Dawn called. I thought she was hurt at the bottom of the hill," Sophie said.

"I figured. So you went out into the storm."

The gathered tears began to fall. "I didn't mean to risk the baby, Jake. I just didn't know what to do."

His eyes glowed dark pools of emotion. "The baby? You think I'm concerned for the baby?"

"Yes," she said miserably.

"I'm concerned for you. Don't get me wrong, the baby means the world to me. But there isn't any world without you," he said.

Her heart leapt. "What?"

"I love you, Soph. I don't want this life without you in it," he said.

Her mind swirled while heat bloomed in her chest. "I don't understand."

"I thought about it. The whole time you were out. We can live in San Francisco and visit Montana as much as possible. Maybe even get a summer place here." Jake almost smiled.

"You'd move to the city? With Leila?" she gasped.

He nodded. "I could make enough money in the city to easily travel back and forth. Our kids could have the best of both worlds."

Hope exploded within her entire body. "You'd give up your job with the tribe?"

He exhaled deeply. "I'd have to."

"The best of both worlds?" she asked, her heart spinning.

"Yes," he said.

"Well then." She smiled, her heart in her throat. "Maybe we should live here and visit the city whenever possible."

He frowned. "I don't understand."

"My children are going to grow up with grandparents. And uncles. And meddling friends. Not alone like I did." This was her decision, and she was making it.

"The law and the ranch keep me really busy. I don't know how often we'll be able to travel." His eyes veiled as if he didn't want to get his hopes up.

She loved the stubborn man. "Jake, didn't I tell you? I'm going to be a famous artist. And a golf course designer. Money shouldn't be a problem."

"You're awfully confident, Sunshine." Dark eyes melted to burnt sugar.

"Yeah, I know. By the way, I love you, too," she said.

EPILOGUE

Ten months later

In the background, the band played a soft tune as children romped along the bridges and shrieked with excitement when they spotted swimming koi.

"Willa's Garden is perfect, isn't it, Nathan?" Loni crooned to her grandson while deftly lifting him from Sophie's arms.

"Thanks. Man, he's getting heavy." Sophie stretched her arms over her head before looking around. "Where's my daughter?"

"She's over feeding the koi with Tom. Those fish are going to need a diet by the end of summer." Loni smooched kisses on the baby's nose and then grinned as he giggled. Already, he looked just like his daddy with dark hair and even darker eyes.

Sophie scanned the area. "Okay. Where's my husband? They should be finished posing for the picture by now."

Loni shrugged, her attention focused on the baby's sparkling eyes staring up at her. "I don't know. Probably hanging out with Colton since he's just home for the weekend."

The sound of rapid hooves made both women look toward the main road.

"Oh my!" Loni yelped just as one broad arm leaned down

and lifted Sophie onto a rushing black stallion. Two other horses followed close behind, leaving dust in their wake.

"Jake, for Pete's sake," Sophie bellowed from the rushing horse.

She grasped the silky mane in desperate hands, warmth from the familiar body behind her sending awareness through her stomach.

"Hang on." Her husband's deep voice caused chills down her spine as he maneuvered the large stallion through trees with strong thighs. Thighs that gripped hers while hers gripped the horse.

His strong, oh-so-hard body warmed her as they galloped through the damp woods into a meadow filled with light. The horse skidded to an abrupt stop and birds took to the air. The arm around her waist lowered her gently before her captor leaped lithely to the ground.

She backed up until a tree stopped her retreat.

"She's kinda pretty," said Colton as he stopped his mount.

"She'll do," Quinn agreed gravely. "What are you going to do with her, Jake?"

His eyes remained on the woman watching his approach. "That's my decision," Jake said softly as he stepped forward. "Now go away, both of you."

His brothers turned their mounts and took off.

"One more step, and you'll land on your ass." Sophie lifted her chin, fighting a smile. Shafts of sunlight poked through the pine trees all around them, and a quiet descended in the cool forest.

"Is that a fact?" he drawled while taking another step forward. "Think you can take me?"

"I am pretty tough," she agreed, pressing farther into the rough bark.

"So I have to chase you down to get a second alone with you, hmm? Some captive you turned out to be," he said.

Sophie's mouth watered at the ripple of muscle over her husband's chest. "Not true. I believe we had several minutes together last night. And early this morning."

"True. But between Willa's Garden spring opening, you designing my golf course, and preparing for an art show, by the time my mouth is in your vicinity, it doesn't want to talk," he said.

Love hummed along her veins, through her blood for this man. "It's not my fault you're insatiable."

"Is, too." One final step and he was but a breath away.

Sophie looked up several inches. "You want to talk, huh?"

"Yes, I believe so." A hand fisted in her hair and warm lips dropped to nuzzle her neck.

"Jake, you didn't answer your brother." She tilted her head to allow for better access. "About what you're going to do with me."

His smile was pure sin as he raised his head and midnight dark eyes captured hers. "I caught you, Sunshine. I'm keeping you."

※　　※　　※

READ the next Montana Maverick romance now! Here's a quick excerpt of Under the Covers:

Juliet tensed the second the outside door clanged shut. So much for her brief reprieve. She turned around and sat on the highest rung of the ladder, her gaze on the hard wooden floor so far below her feet. Paintings still hung on the wall, and she needed to take them down. But first, she had to face the sheriff.

She'd known he'd show up after receiving her e-mail. Nerves jumped in her belly as she waited.

He strode into the main room of the art gallery and brought the scents of male and pine with him. Stopping several feet away, he looked up. "Juliet."

"Sheriff." She took a deep breath, trying to keep her focus on his dark eyes.

But that body deserved a second glance. Tight and packed hard, the sheriff wore faded jeans, a dark button-downed shirt, and a gun at his hip. Black hair swept away from a bronze face with rugged features. Not merely handsome, but definitely masculine and somehow tough. Years ago, she'd liked tough. Many years ago.

He cocked his head to the side and studied her.

For months, he'd been studying her...that dark gaze probing deep, warming her in places she tried to control. But Quinn Lodge was all about control, and the smirk he gave promised she'd be the one relinquishing it. "Any other woman, I'd be worried about that top rung. Not you, though," he murmured.

She smiled to mask her instant arousal from his gravelly voice and resorted to using a polite tone. "You don't care if I fall?"

"I care. But you won't fall. You're the most graceful person I've ever met. Ever even seen." Admiration and something deeper glimmered in his eyes.

She swallowed. "Thank you. Now perhaps we should get to the arguing part of the evening."

"I'm not going to argue." Stubbornness lined his jaw, at home and natural along the firm length. "Neither are you."

While the words sounded like a peaceful overture, in truth, they were nothing but an order. She clasped her hands together and smoothed down her long skirt. When he used that tone, her panties dampened. If the boys from the private school who'd dubbed her "frigid virgin" could only see her now. "Good, no arguing. We agree."

His grin flashed a dimple in his left cheek, and he shifted his weight. "You're not leaving the gallery."

"Yes, I am." She should not look. She absolutely would not look. But she'd recognized his move when he's shifted his weight...yes. A very impressive bulge filled out the sheriff's worn jeans.

She swallowed, her ears ringing. Her thighs suddenly ached to part.

His eyebrows rose. "Juliet?"

Guilt flashed through her even as her eyes shot up. "Yes?"

His smile was devastating. "Would you like to finally discuss it?"

"Your erection?" The words slipped out before she could think. *Oh God.* She slapped a hand over her mouth.

He laughed, the sound male and free. "Here in the backcountry, ma'am, we prefer the term *hard-on*. But yes, let's discuss the fact that I'm permanently erect around you. Tell me you're finally ready to do something about it."

Her heart bashed into her rib cage. "Like what?" she choked.

"Well now"—he tucked his thumbs in his pockets, his gaze caressing up her legs to her rapidly sharpening nipples—"I've never taken a woman on a ladder before, but the thought does have some possibilities. How flexible are you, darlin'?"

The spit dried up in her mouth, while warmth flowed through the rest of her. He wasn't joking. If she gave the word, he'd be on her. Shock filled her at how badly she wanted the sheriff *on her*. Most men would be at least a little embarrassed by the tented jeans. Not Quinn Lodge. He wanted to explore the idea.

"While I appreciate your offer, I'd prefer we returned to settling the issue of the gallery." Could she sound any less like a spinster from the eighteen hundreds? "I'm unable to pay the rent, and thus, I need to move on." But where? The upcoming art show needed to be held somewhere close by or nobody would attend. While she had no choice but to flee town right after the opening, at least she could leave on a triumphant note.

"I don't need the rent. Let's keep a running total, and after you're hugely successful, you can pay me." He ran a broad hand through his hair. "Stop being impossible."

She wasn't a charity case. Plus, the last person she wanted to owe was the sheriff. The man viewed the world in clear, unequivocal lines, and she lived in the gray area. A fact he could never know. "I'm sorry, but I'm not taking advantage of you." She was out of money, and no way would she stick around.

He sighed. "Juliet, I don't need the money."

The words from any other man would've been bragging. Not Quinn Lodge. He was merely being nice...and telling the truth. His family owned most of Montana, and he'd invested heavily in real estate. The guy owned many properties, including the two-story brick building that had held her gallery for the past few months, since she'd arrived in town.

She sighed. "I'm not owing you."

His chin lowered.

Hers lifted.

A cell phone buzzed from his pocket. He drew it out, frowned at the number, and then looked back up at her. "I, ah, need to take this. Do you mind?"

"No." Darn if his manners didn't make her feel even more uncomfortable.

"Thanks." He lifted the device to his ear. "Lodge here."

He listened and slowly exhaled. "Thank you, Governor." He shook his head. "I don't think so... Yes, I understand what you are saying." Dark eyes rose and warmed as they focused on Juliet's hardened nipples. She'd cross her arms, but why hide? It wasn't like the sheriff was concerned about the massive erection he was still sporting, and she could be just as nonchalant as he. She dragged her thoughts back to his ongoing conversation.

"I would, but I already have a date." That dimple flashed again, this time longer. "Yes, I'm seeing someone—Juliet Montgomery. She owns the art gallery in town. Of course she'll be at the dance and at the ride. Thank you very much." He slid the phone into his pocket.

Tingles wandered down Juliet's spine. Several of her fantasies regarding the sheriff included being part of his everyday life. Of course, many more centered on his nights. "We're dating?"

"Well now," only a true Montana man could drawl a sentence like that, "how about we reach an agreement?"

She frowned even as her body sprang to attention. Her raging hormones would love to reach an agreement. "I'm not for sale, Quinn."

He lost the smile. "I would never presume you were. Here's the deal—we both need help. How about we assist each other?"

Without knowing the facts, she knew enough to understand this was a bad idea. No matter how many tingles rippled through her abdomen. "Why did you tell the governor we're dating?"

"He tried to fix me up with his niece, and I needed an out. You're my out." Dare and self-effacing humor danced on his face. "How about we date for the next six weeks, just until the election, and you keep the gallery rent-free? You'd really be helping me out."

Quinn was up for reelection for the sheriff's office. She shook her head. "You don't need to play games. Everybody loves you."

"No. The people in the town of Mineral Lake like me. But Maverick County is a large area, and I need the governor's endorsement. The last thing I have time for is campaigning for a job I love when I need to be *doing* that job."

Considering she'd be leaving soon, maybe she should provide him some assistance. "You have more money than the governor. Buy some ads."

"I'm not spending money on ads. It's a waste of resources as well as an insult to hardworking people."

"Tell the governor you aren't interested in his niece." Juliet narrowed her gaze. Quinn Lodge didn't kowtow to anybody.

"Refusing the governor is a bad idea." He stalked closer to the ladder. "His niece is Amy Nelson, a woman I briefly dated, and she wanted more. Her daddy is Jocko Nelson, and he's more than willing to spend a fortune backing Miles Lansing for sheriff. My already dating somebody saves my butt, sweetheart."

The last thing she wanted to talk about was his fine butt. Nor did she want to think about him dating some other woman. "I'm not your solution."

"Besides," he reached the bottom of the ladder and held up a hand, "aren't you tired of dancing around this? For the last few months, we've danced around this."

"That's what responsible adults do." She automatically took his hand to descend.

Electricity danced up her arm from his warm palm.

"Bullshit." He helped her to the hard-tiled floor. "You feel it, too."

Yes, she did, and the crass language actually turned her on. But he didn't know her, and he wouldn't like her if he did. "I've chosen not to act on any temporary attraction." As a tall woman, it truly unnerved her when she needed to tilt her head back to meet his gaze. "How tall are you, anyway?"

He shrugged. "Six four, last time I checked. How about you?"

"Five ten."

He nodded. "Petite. Very petite."

The man was crazy. She tugged her hand free. "I'm not dating you."

"I know. We're pretending." He glanced around at the many paintings on the wall. "Are these from Sophie's new collection?"

"Yes." The man already knew his sister-in-law's paintings adorned the walls.

"Didn't you promise her an amazing showing for the opening of your gallery?" he asked.

Oh, guilt wasn't going to work. Juliet sighed. "Yes."

"Well, then. This is the only place to have an amazing showing, right?" he asked.

Wasn't that just like a man to go right for the kill? Sophie was Juliet's friend, one of her only friends, and the showing meant a lot to her. "You're not being fair."

He reached out and ran a finger down Juliet's cheek, his gaze following the motion.

Heat flared from his touch, through her breasts, right down between her legs. "Stop," she whispered.

His hand dropped. "I need a pretend girlfriend. You need to keep the gallery open. This is a perfect agreement."

Darn it. Temptation had her glancing around the spectacular space. Three rooms, all containing different types of Western art, made up the gallery. The main room already held most of the paintings created by Sophie Lodge. Rich, oil-based paintings showing life in Maverick, life on the reservation, and the wickedness of Montana weather. The showing would put both Sophie's art and Juliet's gallery on the Western-gallery map just like the C. M. Russell Museum in Great Falls, or the National Museum of Wildlife Art in Jackson Hole.

She wanted to be on that map. Perhaps badly enough to make a deal with the sheriff. Plus, she was tired of trying to ignore her attraction to Quinn. Would that attraction explode or fizzle if they spent time together? Frankly, it didn't matter. She had to leave town soon. Why not appease her curiosity? "Okay, but keep your hands to yourself."

"But—"

"No." She pressed her hands on her hips. The man was too dangerous, too tempting. A woman had to keep some control, or Quinn would run wild. No question. "You're creative, and this is your idea. If we pretend to date, you keep your hands off me."

His eyes dropped to an amused, challenging expression. He held out both hands, palms up. "Tell you what. These hands won't touch you until you ask nicely. Very nicely."

"That will never happen," she snapped.

His left eyebrow rose. "I wondered if that red hair came with a temper." Interest darkened his eyes to midnight. "So much passion locked up in such a classy package. I thought so." He leaned into her space. "Be careful, or I'll make you beg."

She almost doubled over from the spike of desire that shot through her abdomen. How many pairs of high-end panties had she gone through the last month, anyway? "Back away, Sheriff."

He stepped back, as she'd known he would, but the confident desire in his eyes didn't wane. He glanced at his smartphone. "Give me your cell number in case I can't find you at the gallery."

She shuffled her feet. A cell? Yeah, right. Even if she had the money, they were too easy to trace. "I, ah, don't have one."

Watchful intelligence filled his eyes as he glanced up. A cop's eyes. "Why not?"

"I have not had time to find the right one and choose a plan," she lied.

"Interesting." He slipped the phone into his pocket, turned on the heel of his cowboy boot, and headed for the door. "Be ready at six tomorrow night for the Excel Foundation Fundraiser in Billings. The drive will take us an hour."

All tension disappeared from the room as he left. Well, except for the tension at the base of her neck from the land line phone being silent. It had been ringing for almost a week with nobody being on the other side. Surely it was a bunch of kids just goofing off, but she couldn't shake the uneasy feeling that kept her up at night. Well, when erotic images of a nude Quinn Lodge weren't haunting her dreams.

She sagged against the ladder as she forced herself to relax.

Yeah, right. Pretending to be the sheriff's girlfriend would be anything but relaxing. What in the world had she just done?

Read Now: Under the Covers

SERIES' LIST

I know a lot of you like the exact reading order for each series, so here you go as of the release of this book, although if you read most novels out of order, it's okay.

MONTANA MAVERICK SERIES

1. Against the Wall
2. Under the Covers
3. Rising Assets
4. Over the Top

KNIFE'S EDGE, AK SERIES

1. Dead of Winter
2. Thaw of Spring

THE ANNA ALBERTINI FILES

1. Disorderly Conduct
2. Bailed Out

3. Adverse Possession
4. Holiday Rescue novella
5. Santa's Subpoena
6. Holiday Rogue novella
7. Tessa's Trust
8. Holiday Rebel novella
9. Habeas Corpus

LAUREL SNOW SERIES

1. You Can Run
2. You Can Hide
3. You Can Die
4. You Can Kill

GRIMM BARGAINS SERIES

1. One Cursed Rose
2. One Dark Kiss

DEEP OPS SERIES

1. Hidden
2. Taken novella
3. Fallen
4. Shaken novella (in Pivot Anthology)
5. Broken
6. Driven
7. Unforgiven
8. Frostbitten

Dark Protectors/Enforcers/1001 DN

1. Fated (Dark Protectors Book 1)

STOPE PACKS (wolf shifters)

1. Wolf
2. Alpha
3. Shifter

SIN BROTHERS/BLOOD BROTHERS

1. Forgotten Sins
2. Sweet Revenge
3. Blind Faith
4. Total Surrender
5. Deadly Silence
6. Lethal Lies
7. Twisted Truths

SCORPIUS SYNDROME SERIES

Scorpius Syndrome/The Brigade Novellas

1. Scorpius Rising
2. Blaze Erupting
3. Power Surging - TBA
4. Chaos Consuming - TBA

Scorpius Syndrome Novels

1. Mercury Striking
2. Shadow Falling
3. Justice Ascending
4. Storm Gathering
5. Winter Igniting
6. Knight Awakening

REDEMPTION, WY SERIES

1. Rescue Cowboy Style (Novella in the Lone Wolf Anthology)
2. Rescue Hero Style (Novella in the Peril Anthology)
3. Rescue Rancher Style (Novella in the Cowboy Anthology)
4. Book # 1 launch - subscribe to my newsletter for more information about the new series.

WHAT TO READ NEXT

I often get asked what book or series of mine people should read first. All books are in written in past tense except for the Grimm Bargains books, which are in present tense. All of my books, regardless of genre, have some suspense and humor in them—as well as romance, of course. They're all fairly sexy romances except for the Laurel Snow thrillers and the Anna Albertini Files.

ROMANTIC SUSPENSE SERIES:

Deep Ops:

This series is about a ragtag group of misfits at Homeland Defense that create a team with each member finding love during a suspenseful time. There's a different couple's romance featured in each book with multiple POVs. Their mascots are a German Shepherd who likes to wear high heels because he feels short, and a cat named Cat that likes to live in pockets and eat goldfish. The crackers, not real fish. Probably. The series starts with Hidden and continues on with new books being released every year.

Sin and Blood Brothers:

These seven books are about brothers created in a lab years ago who've gotten free while still being hunted by the scientists and the military man who trained them. They each find love and romance during a suspenseful time. There's a different couple's romance featured in each book with multiple POVs. The first four books are called the Sin Brothers and then the next three are a spinoff called the Blood Brothers. The series starts with Forgotten Sins.

The Scorpius Syndrome:

This is a post-apocalyptic romance series. A bacteria wiped out 99% of the human race. For survivors, it affects their brains, either making them more intelligent, sociopathic, or animalistic. Jax Mercury, ex-gang member and ex-serviceman, returns to LA to create an inner city sanctuary against all of the danger out there, while hopefully finding a cure. Each book is a suspenseful romance between two people told in multiple POVs. The first book is Mercury Striking.

Knife's Edge, Alaska

These feature four brothers who've returned to their small Alaskan town in the middle of nowhere. Each book features the romance of one of the brothers along with a suspenseful situation that's solved by the end. The books are told in multiple POVs. The first book is Dead of Winter.

Montana Mavericks:

These books are set in Montana in a small town with a bit of suspense in each one. The romance is the focus of these, and there's some good humor. This is a band of brothers type of romance with a very involved and rather funny family. They'd be considered category romances and have dual POVs. The first book is Against the Wall.

Anna Albertini Files:

I wasn't sure where to categorize these stories. They're more woman's fiction or even chick lit with small town hi-jinx as Anna solves a case each time. She has a very meddling family and ends up in very humorous situations while solving cases as a lawyer. In the first book, it appears she has three potential love interests (but only ends up with one), and by the second book, the love interest is obvious and develops each book. Fans love him. This is told in Anna's POV in first person, past tense. The first book is Disorderly Conduct.

There are Christmas novellas as well, each featuring one of the Albertini brothers' romance, and these are told in multiple POVs and third person. The first Christmas novella is called Holiday Rescue.

Redemption, Wyoming Series:

This one features a group of men from around the world who were kidnapped and forced to work as mercenaries for years. They escaped and have made their way to Wyoming, trying to live normal lives as ranchers with a clubhouse. Their motto is: If it can be ridden, we ride it. (Meaning horses, snow-mobiles, motorcycles...LOL). So far, the three prequel novellas have been published, and they're each in an anthology. I should have a date for the series launching soon.

ROMANTIC THRILLER SERIES:

The Laurel Snow Thrillers

These feature Laurel Snow, who's an awkward genius and profiler now working out of her smallish Washington State home with a team - many readers love the secondary characters as well. There's a slow burn romance with Fish and Wildlife Officer Huck Rivers, and each book involves a case. There are different POVs in this one, and a really fun antagonist who readers love to hate. The first book is called You Can Run.

PARANORMAL ROMANCE SERIES:

The Dark Protectors
This series launched my career and is still going strong. The main characters are brothers who are vampires at war with other species. The vampires, demons, shifters, witches, and Fae are all just different species. They can go into sunlight, eat steak, and quite enjoy immortality. They only take blood in fighting or sex. There are fated mates, and once they mate, it's forever with a bite, brand, and sex. They can't turn anybody into a different species, so vampire mates don't turn into vampires, but the mating process increases a human's chromosomal pairs so they get immortality. The first book is called Fated. There's a spinoff that's really part of the main series, and the first book is called Wicked Ride. Then there's a great entry point for the series (a new arc) called Vampire's Faith. Each book in these features a new couple and is told in multiple POVs.

Stope Pack Wolf Shifters
This is a paranormal series featuring wolf shifters set in Washington state. It's sexy and fun. The first two books feature the same couple, and the rest of the books feature a new couple's romance. These are told in dual POVs, and the first book is called Wolf. Yeah, it's kind of on point. LOL.

DARK ROMANCE SERIES:

Grimm Bargains
This is a dark romance series featuring retellings of fairy-tales set in the modern world. Through time, four main families have learned to exchange health and vitality with certain crys-

tals, and in today's day and age, they use these crystals to power social media companies. They have mafia ties. This series is in first person, present tense - told from various POVs. It's my only present tense series. It is dark (not hugely dark compared to some of the dark romances out there), so check the trigger warnings. The first book is called One Cursed Rose, and it's a dark retelling of Beauty and the Beast.

ABOUT THE AUTHOR

New York Times, USA Today, Publisher's Weekly, Wall Street Journal and Amazon #1 bestselling author Rebecca Zanetti has published more than eighty novels and novellas, which have been translated into several languages, with millions of copies sold worldwide. Her books have received Publisher's Weekly, Library Journal, and Kirkus starred reviews, favorable Washington Post and New York Times Book Reviews, and have been included in Amazon best books of the year.

Rebecca has ridden in a locked Chevy trunk, has asked the unfortunate delivery guy to release her from a set of handcuffs, and has discovered the best silver mine shafts in which to bury a body...all in the name of research. Honest. Find Rebecca at: www.RebeccaZanetti.com

Made in the USA
Monee, IL
29 March 2025

14843593R00135